SOMETHING BEGINNING

WITH

'More than a hundred poets combine their talents to give us this exquisitely produced anthology, with dazzling illustrations ... poems playful, poems profound' THE IRISH TIMES

'The poems are written for children, which suits all of us. Buy it for your favourite niece. Keep it for yourself.' OLIVIA O'LEARY

'This is a rich anthology that slips easily between dreamy dimensions, backyard normality, death and humour.' THE IRISH TIMES

'A dream for parents hoping to inspire a love of poetry, and a book that will never be outgrown.' IRISH INDEPENDENT

'Delightful and knowing, tender and mocking ... utter delight.' IRISH CATHOLIC

'Beautifully produced, written and illustrated.' VILLAGE

'Is álainn an leabhar é agus beidh sult le baint as go ceann na mblianta.' LÁ

'If some word-gobbling wizard came and snatched all the poems out of this anthology it would still be a pleasure to browse through. Every page is a dramatic, often zany display of characters, creatures and tumbling objects, all in spectacular colours.' THE IRISH TIMES

SOMETHING BEGINNING

P WITH

NEW POEMS FROM IRISH POETS

EDITOR: SEAMUS CASHMAN

ILLUSTRATORS: CORRINA ASKIN AND ALAN CLARKE

TYPOGRAPHICAL ILLUSTRATIONS: EMMA BYRNE

THE O'BRIEN PRESS
DUBLIN

CONTENTS

... EYE SPY ...

... SOMETHING BEGINNING ...

EDITOR'S INTRODUCTION

'**I** am a house where a litter of poets can slurp up their words noisily,' writes one poet here; and it is my wish that all the readers of this book will abandon good manners and muck in, slurp away noisily, happily, repeatedly, at what these poets have dished up. For in here is a maze of poem-filled words, juggling with ideas and images, filled with laughters, sadnesses and wonders; throughout all is a kind of madness — the madness of being alive to the discoveries of the mad mad worlds around and within us — worlds that can be mined, hacked, sifted, shovelled and reshaped endlessly. And through the enjoyment this can give, beauty will flow, diamonds will sparkle, poems will be absorbed.

I enjoyed commissioning the poems for this collection more than I could have imagined. That legendary standing army of Irish poets, famous, infamous and unknowns, proved, much to my relief, to be more a wild bunch, good-humoured professionals, ready to have a go. And those who had to pass on this occasion were fulsome in their praise of the publisher's concept — to commission one hundred 'new poems for young readers' from Ireland's poets. Those one hundred poems are here, plus another dozen!

Bar a handful that sneaked past me early in the morning, none of these poems saw the light of day before now. For instance, one was printed by some students on a T-shirt in America; another hung out at a hotel in Maastricht! One was on a memorial card. Some more were whispered at poetry readings, and a happy few hid restlessly in poetry wallets waiting for this day. One funny political poem I simply had to revive for this collection. All the rest were specially made for this book — made as a challenge accepted, a gamble that the Muse would send some verses, a PQ test (*Poetry Quotient* — not in your dictionary, but go ask somebody!), and in so many instances which I can directly vouch for, the poems here were written (to quote one *Árdfhile*) as gifts 'for the children'.

The resulting stream of dreams and schemes arriving into my letterbox or emailbox was a delight — poems with fun and entertainment singing in their beating hearts, poems of life experience today, city poems and country poems; poems about being children, about parents, about birds, fish and animals, poems inventing games — to play, to say; story poems; new nursery rhymes; nonsense verse. What hobbit-like, or robotic, or dreamsong fantasy world these poets make of the places where they and we live!

I wish you the reader — young, mid-teens and beyond — hours of pleasure and discovery within these pages, and many years of revisiting again.

Seamus Cashman

. . . with my little

Words Are Such Silly Things

(A playpoem, to be read aloud by four players)
Brendan Kennelly

'O.K., you three guys, let's play the game.
What do I spy with my little eye?
I spy with my little eye
something beginning with –
Come on you guys, start guessing.' f.

'Is it a flower?'
'No!'
'Is it a feather?'
'No!'
'Is it a face?'
'No!' 'Is it a foot?'
'No!'
'Is it a fish?'
'No!'
'Is it a first cousin?'
'No!'
'Is it a frog?'
'No!'
'Is it a frown?'
'No!' 'Is it the future?'
'No!'
'O I give up!'
'And I give up!'
'And I give up!'

[*three voices*] 'So tell us what it is?'
'O.K. guys, I'll tell you.

It's a fone.'

12

'A phone! But phone

doesn't begin with f.
Phone begins with p-h.
Phone is P-H-O-N-E.

Don't you know that?'

'No, don't be silly!

If **feather** begins with f
And **face** begins with f
And **foot** begins with f
And fish begins with f
And frog begins with f
Then fone must begin with f.'
'No, phone begins with p-h.'

'Why?'

'I don't know
p-h sounds like f in phone.'

'O silly silly silly
words are such silly things —'
'and words are such beautiful things,
     silly and beautiful
       like Mommy's curly head
     when she tries to persuade me
     to go to bed.'

'What about not and knot?'

'And bread and bred?'
'Or lie and lie?'
'And tide and tied?'
'Or down and Down?'
'Or Clare and Clair?'
'Or hair and hare and Molly O'Hare!'

'O stop it, you guys! Let's play again:
Let me see now. O yes.
I spy with my little eye
Something beginning with — O.'

[*three voices*]
'O no, please! No, please! No! No! No!'
(P.S. And what does my granny love to bake?
A tasty inimitable sin-again cake!)

Dancing
on the Table

Margot Bosonnet

We've got a table
big and square;
we dance on the table
when Mammy's not there.

We've got a table
sturdy and stout;
we dance on the table
when Mammy is out.

We've got a table
and it's able
to be a stage or a mountain top
and underneath is a cave or shop
or the vilest hold of a sailing sloop
where prisoners are chained to the legs by loops.
It's a nomad's tent in the Gobi desert,
it's a snow dugout on the slopes of Everest
in the wildest storm that tries to sweep
us to our deaths,
it's a pothole deep.
It's a caravan trading merchandise,
it's a pond for skating, thick with ice.

We've got a table chipped in patches,
we've got a table with lots of scratches
but it feels so silky when our feet are bare
that we dance on the table and *we* don't care!

We dance on the table
and we clamour and shout;
we dance on the table
till we're all danced out …

14

Hideout

Desmond Egan

not for doubledecker Dublin
would I swop our little river
crossing under the road

the bridge where I sit with friends
the sloping bank down
under leaves to the big stone
where the light is green

down there
the sound of cars changes
the way an ambulance does passing
everything is a bit different
the flicker of a trout
on the water skin

the road of shadowy oaks
makes the quiet quieter

once I ran away there
and never came back

Txt U L8r

Aislinn O'Loughlin

D gr8 ting bout txt msg cnvrs8ns
s dat u cn uz dese abrvi8ns.
U stp splln wrds d wy dat u auta
& drp sum vwls 2, f dat mks d wrd shrta.

Bt wot f ur so bz b/ng dat clvr
u 4gt hw 2 spll nrml wrds al2gdr?
Coz wit all d ltrs & stf dat wre luzn
dnt u tink rdng dis pom wz cnfuzn?

The Recipe for Happiness

Grace Wells

The recipe for happiness in our house
is to take a cup of flour,
add milk, two eggs, a pinch of salt,
and whisk for half an hour.

Then take the creamy mixture
to the steaming frying pan,
ladle little circles in,
as many as you can.

Watch them all turn gold and brown,
then sit down to eat,
sugar and lemon on one side,
pour maple syrup to complete.

'What are we doing yesterday, Granda?'

a nonsense rime

Máire Mhac an tSaoi

'Inis scéal dom, a Dheaideó.'

'Scéal, scéal,
eireaball ar an éan,
láir bhacach bhúi,
searrach ó sí,
Liam 's a mhac,
liaithe ar leac,
mada rua caorach,
     Ó fada ream!
     Ó fada ream!
     Ó fada ream!
Mada rua caorach,
     Ó fada ream!'

'Cad a dhéanfam inné, a Dheaideo?'
'Fé mar a dheineamar amáireach, a mhaicín.'

Old Witch, Young Witch

Mary O'Donnell

The witch up the road is busily cooking,
stirring the cauldron when no-one is looking.

The thick broth is bubbling with frogs' legs and bats,
and glistening, I think, with the tail-ends of rats.

Our neighbour's not ugly, with warts on her nose,
her smile is so sweet, you'd never suppose

that this is a witch, the vilest one ever.
The thing is, you see, she's awfully clever.

She drives to the school gates every day,
with kids of her own who never would say

that their Ma is a tyrant whose tricks are so vast,
(their mouths buttoned shut by some spell she has cast).

She has charmed even them (not to mention the cat),
to stick by her side and not say what she's at!

She offers some kids sweets of poisonous weeds,
that change in our bellies to hard little beads.

She gives jolly parties, pretends to be nice,
but cross her just once and your head's full of lice.

She knows that I know what she's at in the dark,
out on a broomstick, seeking her mark,

hovering close where the bonfires light,
hunting low over fields for children at night.

But now that I'm growing I've spells of my own,
I know how to stop her by holding two bones

from last Sunday's beef dinner, up to the moon
where I cross them and murmur the words of my rune.

This is the season young witches are growing,
learning the trade without OLD witches knowing!

Word Game

Philip Casey

What am I to the sky? say I.

What are you to the shoe? say you

What is he to the flea? says he.

What is she to the Tree? says she.

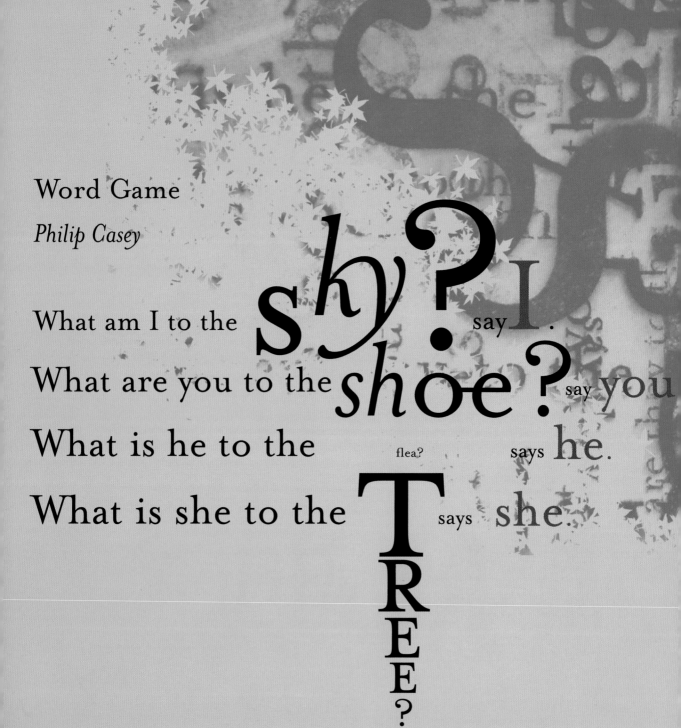

Hoppy New Year:
a one-legged nursery rhyme

Thomas Kinsella

Winter stiff with frosts and freezes.
Spring renews with warming breezes.
Easter sinks us to our kneeses,
Grateful for the griefs of Jesus.
Summer – bright with birds and beeses.
Autumn – leaves forsake the treeses.
Winter, damp with foul diseases,
Rounds in dark: the season seizes.

What are we to the *Sea?* say we.

What are you to the zOO? say you.

What are they to the play? say they.

The Great Blue Whale

Kerry Hardie

Nobody knows
where he goes
nor what he does in the deeps,

nor why he sings,
like a bird without wings,
nor where he eats and sleeps.

The blue whale roves
through watery groves,
his heart is the size of a car,

his tongue, on the scale,
makes zoologists pale –
it's as heavy as elephants are.

A blue whale's vein
without stress or strain
could be swum down by you or me.

He's the biggest feature
that ever did creature
the sky, the land or the sea.

Sruthán sa tSeapáin

Nuala Ní Dhomhnaill

Thíos in íochtar an uisce
snámhann na héisc 'ayu'
go gasta
ar an grinneall.

'Ayu, ayu' a bhéicimíd
go sásta
nuair a chímíd iad.

'Ayu, ayu' a smeachaimíd
go blasta
nuair a ithimíd iad.

23

Belly Buttons
Gabriel Fitzmaurice

An 'inny' or an 'outie' —
a belly button goes
in like Dingle harbour
or out like the Pope's Nose.

The Love Song of
Harry Hippo
Larry O'Loughlin

Harry Hippo fell in love
one Sunday afternoon
and sang his girl friend love songs
beneath the jungle moon.

'Oh, marry me,' sang Harry,
'and I'll cover you in kisses
and be so proud when you become
my hippopotamissus.'

24

Sa Bhaile

Una Leavy

Níl aon tinteán
mar do thinteán féin.

Croch suas do chóta,
bain díot do bhróga,
faigh cupán tae agus
suigh cois na tine.

Cuirtíní dúnta,
seanchlog ag bualadh,
gaoth ins an simléar
ag cogar sa chiúnas.

An cat is an madra
'na gcodladh araon.
Níl aon tinteán
mar do thinteán féin.

An 'inny' or an 'outie' — what kind of one have you? I wish I had an 'inny' 'cos mine sticks out. Boo hoo!

Ar an Seilf sa Leabharlann

Mícheál Ó Ruairc

An raibh tú riamh ann
ar an seilf sa leabharlann?
Bíonn spórt agus spraoi ann
ar an seilf sa leabharlann.
Tá fear a thaistil an domhan ann
ar an seilf sa leabharlann.
Cónaíonn madra rua agus coinín donn ann
ar an seilf sa leabharlann.
Tá file ina chime ann
ar an seilf sa leabharlann.
Tá cogadh agus gorta ann
ar an seilf sa leabharlann.
Tá stair agus tíreolas ann
ar an seilf sa leabharlann.
Tá grá agus crá croí ann
ar an seilf sa leabharlann.
Tá bleachtairí agus bithiúnaigh ann
ar an seilf sa leabharlann.
Tá buachaill bó ar chapall ann
ar an seilf sa leabharlann.
Tá fuirse agus fulaingt ann
ar an seilf sa leabharlann.
Tá éisc ó bhun na habhann
ar an seilf sa leabharlann.
Tá ollphéist le dhá cheann
ar an seilf sa leabharlann.
Tá spiaire ón Rúis ann
ar an seilf sa leabharlann.
Tá taibhse i bhfolach ann
ar an seilf sa leabharlann.
Tá bean sí ar scuab ann
ar an seilf sa leabharlann.

Tá iontaisí an tsaoil ann
ar an seilf sa leabharlann.
Ar mhaith leat cónaí ann
ar an seilf sa leabharlann?

26

Apple Pip

John W Sexton

Into an apple I took a bite
apple pip, apple pip, apple pip
and there she was curled up tight
apple pip, apple pip, apple pip
a fine young woman with night-black hair
apple pip, apple pip, apple pip
what did she do to get in there?
apple pip, apple pip, apple pip
she ran around my fingers twice
apple pip, apple pip, apple pip
her skin was white and cold as ice
apple pip, apple pip, apple pip
I asked her would she be my bride
apple pip, apple pip, apple pip

but she brusquely pushed me to one side
apple pip, apple pip, apple pip
oh no dear sir, she said to me
apple pip, apple pip, apple pip
unless you retrieve from the cold dark sea
apple pip, apple pip, apple pip
these three things I tell you of
apple pip, apple pip, apple pip
and only then can I be your love
apple pip, apple pip, apple pip
first of all the salt in the sea
apple pip, apple pip, apple pip
every grain you must bring to me
apple pip, apple pip, apple pip
and when you have completed that task
apple pip, apple pip, apple pip
this is the next one I will ask
apple pip, apple pip, apple pip
bring me some water that isn't wet
apple pip, apple pip, apple pip
but you won't be quite finished yet
apple pip, apple pip, apple pip
between the water and the sand
apple pip, apple pip, apple pip
collect all the seashells in one hand
apple pip, apple pip, apple pip
when she had finished my apple was gone
apple pip, apple pip, apple pip
and then she vanished and so has my song
apple pip, apple pip, apple pip

Training the Robin

Dermot Healy

One day the robin landed at last
on Jimmy's outstretched foot

and so he kept his shoe where it was
for fear of frightening the bird

and she perched there a while
then flew off.

Tuesday he sat down outside
on the fish box

and the bird landed again
on the toe of his shoe

and this time she sang once
before taking off.

Next day she was waiting for him
when he came out.

He crossed
his legs

and she sat on his shoe
for an hour

and pertly sang
looking toward him,

jumped down,
back on, and sang;

tipped to the sill
to his shoe;

and so it went on
till the stiffness in his foot grew

and the next time
she left him

he stood up
and shook himself.

But the bird, growing bolder,
landed on his shoulder;

now he could not sit down for fear
of giving offence to the bird

so the two of them stood
some time together.

She went quiet,
so quiet he couldn't tell if she was there

till he coughed
and the robin took off.

He turned to the door
but just before

he stepped in
for the night

she landed on his cap
in the half-light

turned around
around on his head

then suddenly rose
and shot round the gable.

The day
was over.

He sat by the table
for half-an-hour of radio

washed up
the cup

put by
his listening tools

his cap
his shoes

and then he slept
where sleep is kept.

The Creatures' Crazy Jamboree

Michael Smith

The cat danced with the fiddle,
the dog jumped on the drum,
the mouse blew on the whistle,
on the guitar the budgie strummed.

The hamster wheeled his treadmill
as if he was going to die;
the rabbit pricked up his ears,
the spider waltzed with the fly.

The woman sat in her armchair,
watching the creatures play;
the man snored in the corner,
tired from his work that day.

The hen came in from the yard
to join in the musical fun;
the sly old fox crept through the window;
he said he hated the sun.

The cow mooed on the bugle,
the horse neighed the trombone;

the magpie read the musical score
and the robin danced on a stone.

The donkey brayed on the trumpet,
the raven chanted in prayer;
the owl hoo-hooed down the chimney
and gave all the creatures a scare.

The bluebottle buzzed on the table,
frightening the flies away;
the butterfly flapped on the lettuce
the worms had nibbled that day.

The snake slid out from the skirting
and wriggled a belly-dance;
the woman stared at these antics
and thought she was in a trance.

But things ended abruptly
when the man woke out of his sleep;
he said he was having a nightmare
and the house was full of sheep.

The woman told him not to be silly,
there was only the dog in the house;
and the dog agreed with the woman
and called the man a mouse.

Cold Day, Hot Day

Joan McBreen

On a cold day
three sparrows
sit together
on the telephone wire,
heads close
to their chests.

On a hot day
three fishes
play —
oh, the fun they have
in the cool caves
beneath the sea.

Three caterpillars
crawling on the wall
take fright
when a voice
says, 'that's tickly!'

Three

Peter Fallon

1
Was it a backroad near Blacklion
where we watched them waiting to be milked, a herd
of pandas congregating by an iron gate?

2
He is learning about the birds,
the bees, and other things:
They're 'flutterbyes'.
And they? They're 'flapwings'.

3
As we drive past the mines
Adam says to me:
They're working hard
in the cloud factory.

Líadan

a poet of the seventh century

Susan Connolly

Five main roads converge at Tara,
monks live on tiny islands,
Newgrange lies tumbledown.

Líadan and Cuirithir hear
the lulling song of the forest,
the roar of a flame-red sea.

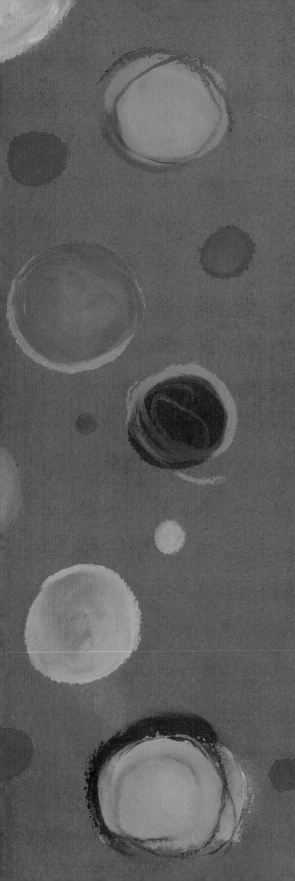

Dorothy's Dotty Dress

Vona Groarke

I'd like you to meet my niece, Dorothy Dooley.
Today she would like us all to call her *Julie*.
I've told her that *Julie Dooley* sounds strange
but she says to me: 'Well, I fancy a change!'

Here's Dorothy's mother – her name is Jean:
on dresses and dotty things, she's very keen.
Now, Dorothy (although she could not be sweete
wears only old denim and a brown windcheater.

Now, Dorothy's dungarees are *very* cool,
brilliant for climbing the big tree at school.
They never get dirty, well hardly ever,
though Dorothy wears them in all kinds of weath

They have pockets and buckles and no awkward z
good places to hide all those ribbons and clips
that Jean does her hair in, to make her look pret
though Dorothy thinks that she looks plain old t

Dorothy likes all her clothes to be dark
and nothing her mother might whisper or bark
can get her to even try on a bright colour.
Dorothy always says: 'I want it *duller*.'

So imagine when Jean brings home her surprise
Dorothy just can't believe her two eyes,
her mother had bought such a *horrible* gift,
Dorothy knew she was right to be miffed.

She'd been hoping for lego, a puzzle at least
or some frightful tale of a horrible beast
that eats girls in dresses and nice shiny shoes
but instead, guess what *Mother* decided to choose

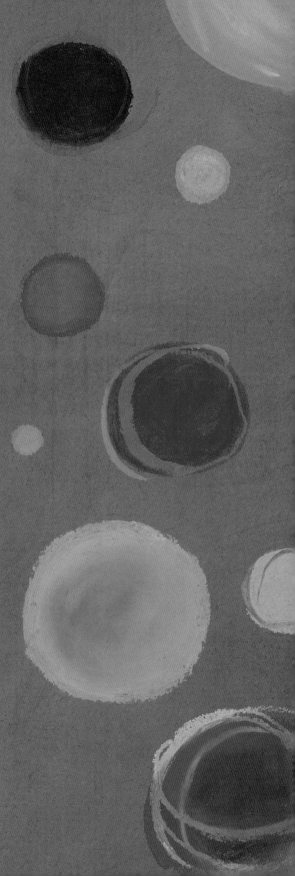

Oh no, it's exactly what Dorothy dreaded
and our little friend, she came right out and said it:
'It's *yucky*, you must know I'll *never* wear this,
it's not dark, it's not trousers: it's … it's a *dress*.

And worse, it's all purple and covered with dots,
it looks like it's having a bad dose of spots.
I swear I won't wear it, so don't even try,
If you bring it near me, I'll scream and I'll cry.'

Jean said, 'Now Dorothy, don't be so mean,
those old dungarees aren't fit to be seen.
You've a party on Sunday, you should look your best.
So say nothing else, *'cos you're wearing that dress.'*

Dorothy said, 'Mum, I just can't believe
that you'd buy me a dress that has big lacy sleeves.
And there's one other reason I hate this dress lots,
why I never will wear any clothes that have dots.'

Dorothy doesn't want her birthday spoiled
by a horrible dress and two horrible boys.
Well they're not really nasty, but they are really *boys*
and Dorothy knows that they'd really enjoy

to be calling her 'Spotty Dot' all through the day
and to have them all laugh at her. Oh no. *No way.*
So our little Dorothy thinks up a plan
that she shares with no-one, specially not Jean.

So what did she do, little Dorothy Dooley?
I have to confess to you, really and truly
I haven't a clue what she did with the dress,
but I know what the minx did to Jean and myself.

She locked us both into the bathroom together
and said, 'You two relax in there. Please do not bother
your heads about *us*, you know we'll be fine.
I'm sure we'll be having a fabulous time.

Now, don't worry, I'll let you back out at six
and I'll save you some birthday cake, so you won't miss
anything really, except maybe the sight
of me in my spotty dress, *looking a fright*.'

With that, she laughed and ran off down the stairs
and all afternoon, we heard laughter and cheers
coming up from the garden, but what we did not
hear was anyone even once calling her 'Dot'.

She never came back, though we thumped and we roared,
until they had gone. Then she opened the door.
And what do you think she was wearing for us?
The purple dress — clean as a whistle, of course!

Doggerel for Emily

Richard Murphy

There was a dog
who was a mug,
he said what a soggy
doggy
says on a muggy
day, with a wag
of his wiggly juggly tag
of a tail.

A hag
came out of a bog
with a big bag
to catch the dog,
so he dug
his fangs in her wig,
she wriggled into a log
and that mug of a dog
sat on it barking
'Slug, slug.'

Síofra Sí

Celia de Fréine

Bíonn Síofra Sí
sióg na bhfiacla
ag obair léi
gach uile oíche

ag eitilt go tapaidh
ó theach go teach
ag bailiú fiacla
go cúramach

ag lóisteáil airgid
faoi bhun piliúr
ag bronnadh sonais
gach uile uair

ag brostú abhaile
le breacadh an lae
ag súil go mór
lena cupán tae.

Hallowe'en

Michael Longley

It is Hallowe'en. Turnip head
Will soon be given his face,
A slit, two triangles, a hole.
His brains litter the table top.
A candle stub will be his soul.

37

Robot Kid

Patrick Chapman

Imagine being built with bolts
and powered by a million volts.
You'd have to wear a glove to shake
the hands of other kids — or make

them disappear in puffs of smoke!
And then you'd have to play and joke
with different children every week
because your friends were always — Eek! —

exploding, until one smart kid
unplugged you from the power grid.
And then you'd sleep for evermore,
your only sound, a robot snore.

So thank your lucky, lucky stars
and some small planets, that you are
a kid of flesh and blood — and not
a super-voltage kid robot.

Santa's Poem

Sean Clarkin

The dogs in the streets were surprised, not impressed,
by this apparition funnily dressed.

The children standing half-in the hall
knew the night that I would call.

I rang my bell and announced the news:
(Was I really in Santa's shoes!)

'Everybody has his burden to bear,'
the butcher laughed as I passed his door.

I was Town Crier from far away.
Message and Messenger for one day.

Lifting his cap to reveal his hair
Dunphy the Postman crossed the floor.

By Michael Street I was growing red.
'SANTA'S IN TOWN' the poster said.

I was tickly and sweaty and awfully sore
(the big boots) when I reached the store.

They laughed or loved me for many an hour
those children who now are fewer and fewer.

Box Beneath the Bed

Sara Berkeley

Searching for a missing mitten
way in underneath the bed
among the dust-rolls big as Britain —
Hey! what's this box you've found instead?

A box is such a mystery
you're filled with sweet anticipation
the thrill of possibility,
promise, hope, and expectation.

Just think: it might hold anything
that fits inside an empty box,
rubber bands or bits of string,
socks or locks or blocks or rocks.

Threads and needles, thimbles, wool,
pine cones, leaves, or acorns round,
feathers, chestnuts, shells so full
of washing, wavelike, seaside sound.

Doll-house cups and silverware,
so that's where all my marbles went!
baby teeth or locks of hair,
a glass you cracked, a coin you bent.

Pushpins, paper clips, and tacks,
pens and pencils, brushes, inks,
buttons, beads, or ribbon scraps,
single earrings, missing links.

The cards you used as fortune-teller
a rolling eye, fake fingernails,
the spoon you bent as Uri Geller,
a tiny book of fairytales.

Postcards, letters, foreign stamps,
sprigs of roses from a hat,
matchbox cars with racing ramps,
scribbled names: now who was that?

Flashlights, key rings, bookmarks, maps,
jigsaw puzzle pieces lonely,
corks and labels, bottle caps,
striped shoelaces (one lace only).

Maps of treasure, crystals, whistles,
screws or nuts or bolts or plugs,
toothbrushes with flattened bristles,
curled-up spiders, ew! dead bugs.

Rubber stamps and calculators,
staples, straws, and glue, and glitter,
tiny plastic alligators,
patterns for the hopeful knitter.

Magic markers, lollipop sticks,
lego, dice, stray dominoes,
silly glasses, magic tricks,
bouncy balls and Duncan yo-yos.

hairgrips, scrunchies, butterfly clips,
knobs and switches, dials and hooks,
tissues, sunscreen, balm for lips,
lists of favourite films or books.

Library cards and treasure-hunt clues,
band aids, batteries, elastic,
ticket stubs from fairs and zoos,
photographs of trips fantastic.

A box might turn up things you lost,
or hid or saved or thought you sold,
a piece of childhood used and tossed
aside because you grew too old.

Or maybe what you have is just
a box of nothing, rich and rare,
a space filled up with magic dust
and hopes and dreams and quiet and air.

The first giraffe to be forced to live in a shoe

Dermot Bolger
(Aged 44 & three quarters)

I'd like a tall spacious house, wouldn't you?
With wooden doors and floors and curtains of blue,
a Turkish bath with gold taps spraying bubbly goo,
and, on the roof, a spacecraft with seating for two.

So can anybody anywhere under the sun,
tell me exactly where I went wrong?
My name is Terrence Twitchy Tightfit McHugh
the first giraffe to be forced to live in a shoe.

It is entirely my own fault I have to confess,
I jumbled up the advertisement into a mess,
and imagined it read 'Dream-homes exceeding nice',
instead of 'Dwellings suitable for exceeding small mice'.

I paid my deposit and they gave me a key,
I did not find my house, my house found me.
While scanning the street to spy which mansion was mine
I stumbled over a shoe with a Sale Agreed sign:

'Reserved for Terrence Twitchy Tightfit McHugh
the first giraffe to purchase a size-nine shoe.'
My life is not so bad since I've adjusted to it,
annoying relations never visit because they can't fit.

And all of my neighbours are exceeding nice,
twice a day I'm infested by friendly mice,
and by a hippo who visits and eats all my soap
while his son takes my shoelaces as a skipping rope.

He tells me about an elephant living with a fox
half a mile from here in a disused match box
and how every night in Africa each rhinoceros
queues up at the water hole for his fish and chips.

He's an impossible liar and a tremendous rogue,
and says he envies my space compared to his wee abode
with its seven sunken baths and vast staircase.
He says it is exhausting to own so much space.

But he never asks me home in case I eat his soap
or commandeer his washing line as a skipping rope.
He wanders off for his tea with his youngest son
who invariably leaves the laces of my house undone.

Can anybody anywhere under the sun,
tell me exactly where I went wrong?
My name is Terrence Twitchy Tightfit McHugh
the first giraffe to be forced to live in a shoe.

Is This What I Get For?

Patrick Cotter

My teeth are all stuck,
they're covered in muck:
is this what I get for
eating chewing-gum bars?

My eyes have turned green,
my brows have gangrene:
is this what I get for
seeing jungley stars?

My legs are all smelly
and feeling like jelly:
is this what I get for
wearing waffley boots?

My nose is like putty,
my nostrils all smutty:
is this what I get for
sniffing pigsty rain-chutes?

My ears are all woolly
and stretched by a pulley:
is this what I get for
hearing baddy-witch FM?

My fingers are disappearing,
flickering and reappearing:
is this what I get for
touching a ghosty coat's hem?

SAD

Larry O'Loughlin

It's sad to think
that lots of toys
that moms and dads
buy girls and boys
are made by
little girls and boys
who never get
to play with toys

Do you know what the sea is able to do?

Pat Ingoldsby

Do you know what the sea is able to do?
For all of her millions and billions and trillions of tons,
her rocks and her wrecks, her seaweed and stones,
her mermaids and serpents, mysterious bones,
her tempests to test you, fish that can fly,
pinkeens that are gone in the wink of an eye,
whirlpools to suck you as if you're a sweet,
sharks who would shred you like yesterday's wheat,

do you *know* what the sea is able to do?

She is able to lie perfectly still
without uttering a sound,
quiet as a feather adrift on the ground.

I find that almost impossible to do.
What do you think? ... Me too!

...eye spy

An t-Amhránaí

Gabriel Fitzmaurice

Osclaíonn an t-amhrán
amach ó lár mo chroí.
Is mise an t-amhrán anseo,
is mise an t-amhránaí.

Canaim uaim mo dhóchas,
canaim uaim mo ghrá,
canaim uaim mo sholas,
canaim uaim mo chrá.

Istigh i gcúinne tábhairne
im' aonar, cúl le balla,
in áit a bheith im' *phopstar*
in Amharclann, Páirc nó Halla,

istigh i gcúinne tábhairne
ag canadh dom féin amháin,
is mise an t-amhránaí anseo,
is mise an t-amhrán.

The House that Barks

Cathal Ó Searcaigh

I am a house
with three barking bedrooms
that keep the lurking
nightshadows
at bay

I am a house
with a snout stove
that dribbles
hot slobber
on a winter's day

I am a house
where a hoover in heat
gloats over the floor
sniffs the rumps of cushions
mounts the backs of sofas

I am a house
that lifts the hindleg
of a kitchen tap
to water
a shrub of saucepans

I am a house
with a bristling door
that keeps
the neighbour's tomcat
away

I am a house
that waggles its chimney
affectionately
when its master returns

I am a house
where a litter of poets
can slurp up
their words
noisily

I am a house
that bares the teeth
of its letterbox
to chase away
the letter that says

'Your poem
is not suitable
for our Poultry Magazine'

The North Pole

Frank McGuinness

The ice built that house.
Frozen windows allowed in
what light they could.
Two bedrooms
measuring day by darkness
touched cold and turned
the heart to red
sleet and snow.
Men cried and
women listened.
Women cried and
turned to stone.

In the bare garden
red children played
games of fast and loose,
lucky sods to leave
that path of hardened,
headstrong ground
where nothing grew but
sorest, sourest rock.
Women cried and
men listened.
Men cried and
turned to stone.

Winter froze forever
the kitchen table,
the scullery,
the living room.
Floors turned into
deadly weapons
sharp as silver forks,
red as meat on knives.
Children cried and
learned to listen,
children cried and
turned to stone.

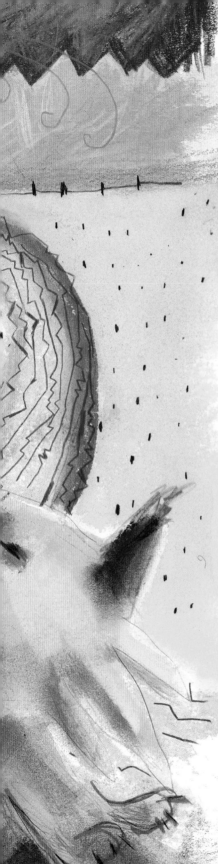

Bunoscionn

Áine Ní Ghlinn

Ar leoithne gaoithe
ar scamall aeir
thuirling cluas mhór ghroí
anuas ón spéir

Sheas i lár an ghairdín is
d'umhlaigh sí go béasach
Chas sí thart go grástúil
is d'fhan sí seal ag éisteacht

le crónán an chait
le búiríl na habhann
le siosarnach na nduilleog
le cogarnaíl na gcrann

leis an madra ag tafann
leis an ngaoth ag feadaíl
leis an mbáibín ag caoineadh
le préachán ag grágaíl

Bhí an luascán ag geonaíl
Bhí an geata ag gíoscán
agus thuas os ár gcionn
bhí seordán eitleáin

Chúb an chluas chuici
Rinne umhlú arís
is cheap mé ar dtús
go raibh sí ar bís

Ansin go tobann
chuala mé gleo aisteach
mar a bheadh fuaimeanna an ghairdín
á gcasadh is á meascadh

Chas an chluas thart
go mall is go réidh
is ar leoithne gaoithe
d'éalaigh sí léi

Fágtha sa ghairdín
bhí an madra ag búiríl
Bhí an luascán ag caoineadh
is an cat ag feadaíl

Bhí an geata ag tafann
Bhí an abhainn ag gíoscán
is ó bhéal an bháibín
chuala mé seordán

Bhí na crainn ag crónán
Bhí an ghaoth ag grágaíl
Bhí préachán ag siosarnach
Bhí eitleán ag geonaíl

D'fhéach mé in airde
Bhí an chluas i bhfad ar shiúl
ach thabharfainn an leabhar
gur chuala mé gáire toll magúil

The Furk

John McAuliffe

The furk's not at all like a grouse,
He smells in fact like a goat
And he noseys about like a mouse
And his feet are as huge as a house
But he floats a bit like a boat.

And he eats nothing else except stew
Which he makes out of spiders and sheep.
And his drink which he drinks from a shoe
Is a frog, egg and rainwater brew
And he snorts and then snores in his sleep.

The furk is a furious kind of a beast.
His nest is a little ice igloo
And he papers his wall with a sort of a glue
That attracts little snowflakes and insects
Which stick to the wall till they're blue.

If ever you see him a-walking the earth
He strides and he slams and he stomps
And he jams and he jerks and he jumps
And he says what he means with great effffort
For his speech has peculiar F-cramps:

56

'I'm the Furk and I own all the ice
And my fnest is a fbeautiful figloo
And I feat fspider fstew and I fdrink from a fshoe
And fpaper the fwalls with fnowflakes and flies
I'm the Furk and I fown fall the fice.'

57

Angel Boy

Maurice Riordan

Angel Boy lives on Fitzroy Road
and goes to Fitzroy Primary School,
where even the teachers call him Gel-Boy.
And no-one knows, not even his Auntie Ajo,
he comes from further off than Somalia.
Much further off – as he knows on warm nights
when he floats above his bunk bed
and wants to slip through the open window
to do somersaults around the city lights.
Knows it on Sports Day when he runs a lap
so fast he must slow up so his mate,
Eddie, can beat him at the tape.
Knows it when little Betty White fell
one whole flight of steps and he couldn't save her,
not without giving away his secret.
Which he must keep till the world is older
and he's called on to do some special job
– maybe to deflect a meteor into space
or to take a test-tube of deadly virus
and bury it on the flip side of the moon.
He doesn't know yet, but it will be dangerous
and important. So he must act like normal.
Well, almost normal. When he runs to school
in his Nike trainers, he keeps his feet
half-a-centimetre above the street.

Skinhead

Mark Granier

My brother had so many hard knocks
he should have stayed in bed.
Instead,
he bought a brand-new pair of *Docs*
and shaved his head.

Street Dancer

Gabriel Rosenstock

There once was a boy who danced on the street,
danced with his arms, danced with his feet.
He danced all day from the sun's first light —
danced with stars in the purple night.
'Nothing to lose!' he cried, 'Nothing to lose!
nothing at all but the soles on my shoes!'
And people would stop and stare a while
shaking their heads with a little smile ...
Sometimes he'd wriggle and sometimes he'd shake —
sometimes he even danced like a snake.
At times he was wild, at times he was tame —
no two dances were ever the same.
He had names for his dances: Falling Snow
was the name of a dance that was terribly slow.
He made up others as he went along:
Polish Goose and Tibetan Gong.
Sometimes he'd chant or sometimes he'd hum —
mostly he just preferred to be stumm.
Was he born to dance? Nobody knows ...
but when he was born he wriggled his toes.
He was dancing as soon as he learned to walk
dancing before he was able to talk.
'Hello, I see you're dancing too!'
he once exclaimed to a shy bamboo.

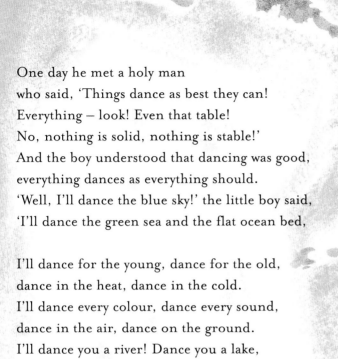

One day he met a holy man
who said, 'Things dance as best they can!
Everything – look! Even that table!
No, nothing is solid, nothing is stable!'
And the boy understood that dancing was good,
everything dances as everything should.
'Well, I'll dance the blue sky!' the little boy said,
'I'll dance the green sea and the flat ocean bed,

I'll dance for the young, dance for the old,
dance in the heat, dance in the cold.
I'll dance every colour, dance every sound,
dance in the air, dance on the ground.
I'll dance you a river! Dance you a lake,
the falling leaves and the crooked rake.
Dance you the whales that roam the sea,
dance you Time and Eternity.
The sickle moon, the planet Mars,
the thousands and thousands and millions of stars!

Yes, I will become the dance,' said he,
'I am the dance, the dance is me!'

Van Gogh's Yellow Chair

Mark Roper

I would love to sit
in the yellow chair
in the painting,

when a shadow lies
like a shy animal
in a corner

and the day's air
is like water in which
small noises swim,

I would light my pipe
and watch
the blue smoke rise,

I would sit there
safe from harm,
safe from all surprise.

Beyond the frame
on every side
the outside world

would open wide,
but I'd have crossed
the great divide.

Nothing could touch me
if I sat there.
I would live forever

so long as I never
rose from
that yellow chair.

Lion King

Joseph Woods

You've been watching the weather
in your Grandad's face
as he sleeps armchaired
in the sitting room

and how the newspaper flopped
to his feet like a seagull
big with wings of newsprint.

Watching the weather in his face
is more interesting than *The Lion King*
and when he wakes from his snooze
he always looks like a spaceman

landed on some strange planet
but still manages a smile
when you ask him, *Grandad
were you old before you were old?*

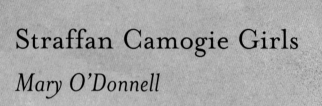

Straffan Camogie Girls

Mary O'Donnell

We are the camogie girls.
Watch us. Fear us. See our hurls.
When the sliotar comes our way,
we dip and curve, up the pace,
grab the ball, toss it high,
till Nessa, our ace, cracks it home.

Jenny's mid-field, good against Ardmore,
who stare with fish faces and never speak.
Teams like them behave like freaks,
then they out-pass so fast, we wish
they'd fall, but they hog the ground,
possession's all. They push us around.

On our side, Tanya the Terrible
tries to pass the sliotar to me and Jade
(away from a girl whose hurl is like a blade).
But she's often in a dither,
or she trips and falls, then sends it wide.
Tanya'd drink blood to play forwards.
I've been one for ages, but my legs
are faster. That sets her in rages.

When we whack the ball into goal
it's like sunshine or Christmas.
We hear the crack of leather on wood,
watch the perfect circling pace
as it blasts into the net like a bullet,
and the other goalie's wailing after Sive
has left her trailing and upset.

Sometimes, we'd kill our own and no mistake,
we're full of hate, not on the field, but after,
in the dressing-room, listening
to the other team's laughter.
Words and stuff flow like blood, as we blame
who wasn't fast enough. Then we make up
by huddling in a ring, raise our hurls
and sing, knowing we'll be back
'cos of this burning in our bellies,
to get even with those nellies from Kildare.

We've lost the last three games.
Four–Two. Three–Nil. Six–Four.
BUT WE ARE THE CAMOGIE GIRLS!
Watch us. Fear us. See our hurls!

Me in a Tree

Julie O'Callaghan

Unfortunately, it wasn't
a luxury tree house
with hot and cold running cocoa
or with a robin

bringing me breakfast in bed.
A squirrel didn't toss acorns
at me when I needed to wake up.
No — that wasn't how it was.

I hid high up in the leaves.
So many thoughts were floating,
I speared them on to twigs
to see them twinkle in the sun.

But now I realise
I named this poem the wrong thing.
It's not me in a tree.
It's the tree in me.

Turns

Siobhan Campbell

Back and forth, over and back,
don't you land on the concrete crack.
That's the line between here and never,
skip on it and you won't go to heaven.

In and out, out and in,
how many times can you vote to win?
Fuss them down to town by train,
then back home to vote again.

Over and back, up and over,
how many leaves in a four-leafed clover?
One two three four,
no, you're wrong, it has one more,
the secret drill curled in the stem
that leaves the clover furl its whim.

Over and back, take up my slack,
one of us has to go to the back.
Gently mind or it skims a whip,
watch the line, jump or trip.
Hold it straight or lose the tack.
Ah, you've slipped the concrete crack.

The run is broke.
The turn is took.
The rope is down
and here's the dark.

Where I Hail From

Julie O'Callaghan

You can't get in your Jeep
and drive to where I come from.
Not yet anyway, kids.
Where I started my adventure
we led a primitive existence
without laptops, microwaves,
picture phones or video games.

Hard to imagine, I admit:
walking around in nerdish clothes
and an uncool pair of shoes.
But we were happy there
watching our black and white TV,
playing with our non-battery-operated toys,
thinking our old-fashioned thoughts.

It is so many light years away
that I need to scour my ancient brain
for any dimly-lit memories of that place.
I get tired just thinking about it.
Every so often I grab a streetlight
and refuse to keep moving.
Not an option.

We all have to move right along.
I pack my bags each morning
for more time travel,
even farther away from where I started.
I am *so* far away now
I can barely see
the galaxy I hail from.

Solar Eclipse

Áine Miller

Today the eclipse,
hugeness of the word,
a countdown to totality
and we take comfort
still something up there
to be wondered at,
something to be filtered through
a pinhole,
a CD.
Commentators on the Beeb
in sun-flowering vests,
laconic, provide
poor correlative
for what happens,
reduce to squiggles
on laptop screens,
or a shrug and a giggle
from schoolgirls at Penzance,
the gamut of experiments,
radio, scientific,
meteorological.
In two black minutes
we're wholly incapable
of escaping the fidgets,
our flash bulbs pop
nervy exclamations
as fire encircles
Mont St Michel,
and what's to remark
but at what speed
darkness races
in and over,
A definite chill

in the air, and the dog
is wise enough not to
howl at this moon
though crickets chirrup
to order, and snowy
owl's eyes widen.
The old dear who held
her Daddy's hand
at the last eclipse
in 1927
refuses jolly comment.
What's behind us
rolls in again
and passes us out.
Though we crank a notch
in arthritic joints
to claw a shadow,
it cannot hold,
cannot be held.
The winking weather man
in his nine o'clock slot
reshows the clip,
a shade streaking
at fifteen hundred
miles per hour,
been and gone
before he'll wink again.

Shane the Shaman

Máighréad Medbh

Who's a rabbit, who's a bear?
Who's a fox and who's a hare?
Who's a tree and who's an eagle on the wing?
Who's a human, who's a cow?
Who's a snake and who's an owl?
Who's a crow and who's an orca who can sing?

Shane the Shaman takes the beating of the earth
to be inside him and his heart begins a drumming
to the rhythm of its humming,
and its whirring and its buzzing
and its chewing and its mooing
and the turning and the churning
and the colours cool and burning,
and the infinite returning
of the sun at every morning …
and the night with all its crooning
and its moody deep blue mooning
and the stars that blaze and shatter
in the infinite dark matter.

He's gone flying, he's gone scrying,
like a seagull wild and crying,
on the waves for silver fishes,
who have eyes that grant you wishes.
If you saw him now you'd wonder
why his body's in a stupor
and he doesn't feel you touch him,
know you're near or hear you talking.

He's gone walking in his mind
to where the spirits and their kind
are in a flurry, and they scurry
when they see his soul is coming.

He will wander in the dark until
a sign appears so stark
that he can't miss it: it's a letter
with a charm to make us better.
He's a postman from the darkness,
where we all have second cousins.
For every one we see here,
there's another, doppelganger,
maybe angels, maybe spirits,
maybe particles of matter.

That's what Shane believes he knows,
like the holy men of old,
when the animals and trees
gave their spirits to the breeze.

Back he's coming to the drumming
and the quiet sound of humming,
to his fingers and his toes,
legs and shoulders, mouth and nose;
to his body's wonder-vessel,
where his mind is in control.
Eyes are opened, here's the message —
maybe healing for your soul.

You can't talk to Shane the Shaman
like you would to other children.
He's been places you can't dream of,
wild and lonely, dark and cold.
He's been off to see great wonders —
moving mountains, talking clouds;

he's met monsters, walked on rivers,
jumped a chasm, led a crowd.
But he's just as good a friend,
plays a game and kicks a ball,
and you might just need his healing
in the summer when you fall.

Who's a rabbit, who's a bear?
Who's a fox and who's a hare?
Who's a tree and who's an eagle on the wing?
Who's a human, who's a cow?
Who's a snake and who's an owl?
Who's a crow and who's an orca who can sing?

Ceist

Rody Gorman

Sea, ceist agam ort,
a chéirseach:
nuair a chasann tú an fonn sin
ar maidin go luath,
an bhfuil tú ag labhairt leat díreach
mar ba dhual do do leithéid a riamh
nó ag tabhairt le taispeáint
d'aon oghaim dom féin?

An Bhóín Dé

Tom Mac Intyre

Thaispeáin tú thú féin –
leigheas is saineolaí –
i lár an leathanaigh bháin.

D'fhágas im ghaírdín thú
is, támáilteach ó dhúchas,
rinneas dearmad ort, a stór,

go dtí gur stopais mo shúil
aréir: tusa ar ais, beo
beathach, i bhfréamhacha taibhrimh
lasair, bé choille, is seoid.

72

The Heron

Rita Kelly

In an air full of river-spray
the heron stands at weir-edge.
Absolutely still,
deadly still,
frozen still.

A small wind ruffles
a few neck feathers;
they are pure white.

His long legs look like twigs.
Her long legs look like twigs.
So thin,
how can they carry this big grey-blue body?

When she sits on her nest
her legs stick out, hang
down, untidy.
It is an untidy kind of nest.
A big clump of twigs
picked and gleaned,
gathered, pushed and shoved
into some form of shape.

But it is still a clump
low enough in the willow tree.

I love that heron,
so often alone,
by the weir,
who climbs up the air
with languid wing
when I come within sight of him.

Oh the tedium of people walking by
just when she has stared that fish to death.
A second before snatching it out of the water
with killer precision.

Once, just once,
I saw him and her together —
of course I never know which of them
stands on the weir —
there were two herons
perched
as if in a Chinese print,
with sweep of tail, and ever-watching eye,
on the bare, mossed, willow tree.
And then there came two more.
Another pair came too and two more as well
all finding spaces for themselves
beneath the clumpy nest.

It was indeed a mighty heron fest.

Gargoyle

Patrick Deeley

I'm here, high up next the roof
of an old cathedral, and if
you glance from a certain spot
(downhill, across the street)

you'll see grass growing
out of my skull, grass-tufts and moss.
At least that's what I ask
you to see, a garland of grass

and moss, and one tiny clot
of red poppy, waving above the grey
monstrosity, me. Instead,
(it always happens this way)

you catch my fissured grin,
my mounded shoulders, dragonesque
of webs and scales, and stop
dead in your tracks. Then

you tell yourself I'm petrified,
being all of stone, and could
never come down. You even recall
(or try to) the centuries

through which I've clung here,
designed to scare away the demons
people believed in. Except
(now that you've moved closer)

I don't cling, I wheel
about frightful of face and ever
so light on my reptilian feet.
Which makes you think maybe

I am the demon. But what
will come spluttering from
my throat – blood or screams
or an ancient garbled song –

is just your imagination.
So look again. These wrinkles
and worry lines, these cracked eyes
trickling wetness, will say

there's something tries to live
in me, gathering particles
of dust as they rise,
gathering even traffic-smoke

and flakes of shed skin,
nourishing wind-blown spores
and seeds, that I may speak to you
one day only in flowers.

Pony Tales

Dennis O'Driscoll

Home from boarding school, the jolly girls in pony books
plan summer hols round junior camps, gymkhanas, country fairs,
set up a course of multi-coloured barrels and bright striped
timber poles for practice in the rail-fenced paddock.

Muck-out, wash-down, tack-up, plaits, saddle-soap, curry-comb.
Father – tweeds, cravat – hitches the horse-box for the county show.
Mother – waxed jacket; hair pins jabbing from her mouth – fastens
entry numbers to twill riding coats, unmuddies jodhpur boots.

Thud of hooves in the practice arena. Picnic hampers in the car park.
Faults made public in a megaphone's no-nonsense tones.
The end-of-round bow to judges when the last brush fence is skimmed.
Impossible ponies tamed. Horse thieves outwitted in the night.

Emergency supplies conveyed to a snowbound neighbour's farm.
Alarms raised on brave cross-country gallops to a vet.
Finally, our heroines are covered in rosettes of glory,
having overcome a nasty rival's guile …

Their future holds sweat-shirted hunter trials, top-hatted
dressage, the swish glamour of the point-to-point ball.
Best of all, they imagine jumping to their country's rescue:
clear rounds clinching victory in the Nations Cup.

Neighbourhood Watch

Anne Le Marquand Hartigan

I know your dog is old and weary
for him his days grow slow and dreary
his legs are stiff, he stops and staggers

his tail now only limply waggers
his eyes, like mine have deepening baggers
but still he does his job for you – deposits

large and juicy poos.

Please, dear Neighbour, do me one favour
it is a point I fain would labour
those doggy shits I do not savour –

dear Neighbour do you care one bit
where your hound-dog does his shit?
Please look beside my garden railings

brown deposits, spied through pailings
squashy, dried or decomposing
other doggies sometimes nosing –

these relics – I do not enjoy. So
with a shovel please deploy
them to some other place –

I dare you sir to show your face
why should I have this disgrace-
full mess around my place?

How dare you, sir, let him totter
you can't care one little jotter
that he poos inside my gate

where my poor foot, when I come late
on doggie excrement does skate —
would you like it on your plate

for breakfast?

Neighbour, I have had enough,
things are getting pretty tough
and so am I.

Halt, dear Neighbour, vengeance rises
I am thinking sweet surprises
dressed in horrid nasty guises

if you do not change your ways.

You will cry and howl for mercy
as my rage comes down to curse ye
my anger getting worse and worsie,

I'm heaping up a tidy pile
getting deeper all the while
I am savouring my bile —

accept this now — my final hit
as in your letter box I fit
about a ton of doggy shit.

The Rabbit

Frank Ormsby

hangs dead behind the door, hind legs strung,
as never in life.
No-one has closed its eyes.

Its lips wince back
as though caught in the act
of twitching a ticklish whisker.

What starts as drip
ends as dried splash
on the *Fermanagh Herald*.

More deeply dead by the hour,
it will be sold
to a man in a Morris Minor.

My father will wrap it tenderly
in his jacket
and smuggle it out to the car.

The Sock Gatherer

Thomas McCarthy

Patient as any four-legged companion, Elvis, our dog
endures the constant traffic of our human house:
day-long he tolerates the noise of X-Box
and PlayStation 2, expletives that follow
a wrong choice of weapon, accidental thumps on the head
that fall from on high in the form of cushions and shoes;
and forgetfulness, our unforgivable human trait –
oh dear! A door closes upon him in heavy rain
and he, unsung hero, as heroic as Tom Crean
retains his composure while turning into a downpipe.
As for meals forgotten, and the sight of his water-bowl
on the wrong side of a locked gate in mid-August,
I don't dare to mention them, his tolerance being saintly.

Except at night. For at night he extracts a small tribute
from our human kingdom. At night he is a tax-gatherer,
moving from room to room while we are still disconnected
from machines, while we are parallel with him –
Neil's best Nike socks, Kate's multi-coloured leggings,
Cathy's best cottons, my own mouldy socks for boots,
one by one (not pair by pair) he drags them to his basket.
There they are hoarded as an honorarium for dogs,
a reward for the faithful; a pillow for his damp nose.

Head Lice

Terry McDonagh

I've had head lice
twice …

Nearly went bananas, I did.
Worse than bad breath, it was.
Good mates defect to
enemy gangs, take the lice
with them and keep on

My things were put
in the freezer
to frostbite the life
out of the geezers …

I cried for my teddy
in his cold, cold cot …

A teacher got lice four times.
The kids went wild and cheered.
The teacher went home …

They get into hair
and into clothes
and onto pillows
and onto car seats
and onto toys
and onto teddies
and onto friends.

They get around …

One kid took
a photo of a louse
and enlarged it.
It looked like a mouse.
A small girl fainted.
Oh, my God!

Some say super lice
that can't be killed
are on the way.

Don't let this happen,

please …

My friend said
her whole class
had head lice
at her last school
and they scratched
and scratched
and scratched

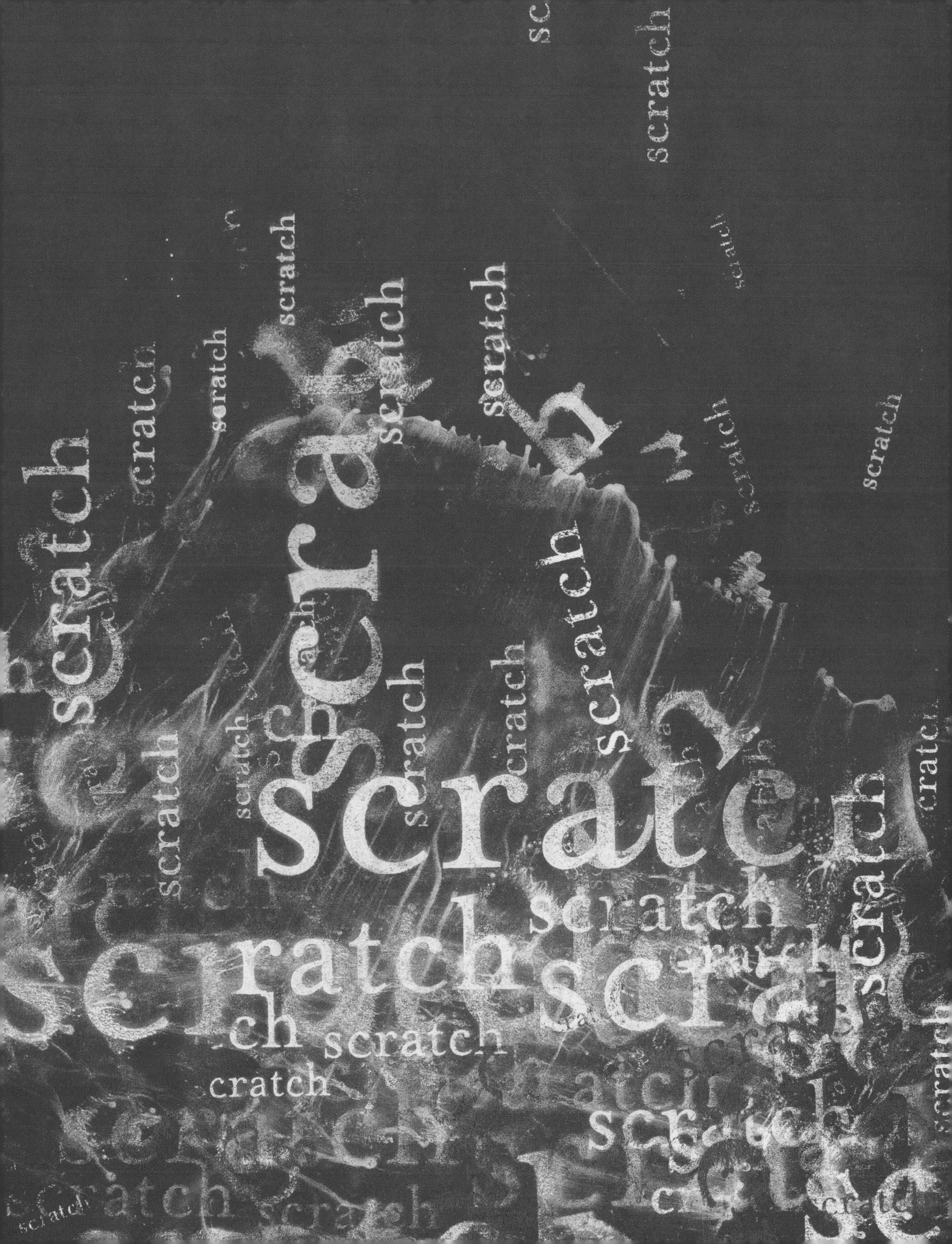
scratch

The Lost Shoe

Eva Bourke

It was freezing, wet and getting dark
when Percepta heard a gentle knock
on the front door and went to look
whoever on earth might
be outside.

She'd never seen anyone anywhere
like the person standing there
in a ragged white cloak, one foot bare,
and on his back two feathery things
like wings

A girl like Percepta didn't need to be told
this was an angel, bedraggled and old
shivering in the December cold
whose toes without shoe
were turning blue.

'*Mia cara*,' said the angel, in a gravelly voice,
'on my way here *j'ai perdu* one of my shoes.
Perhaps you can tell me, if you please,
ist da ein Schuh made of cloud
lying about

stitched and laced with spider thread
and so worn and torn that, *je regrette*,
the nails have long ago fallen out
and its formerly tough fishscale soles
are full of holes?'

Being a practical girl, Percepta replied:
'If I've lost something I usually would
pray to St Anthony or St Jude,
but you, Sir, know them probably
better than me.

Or I try to remember the place where I last
saw or still had the object I lost.'
'Well,' said the angel, 'flying past
Polaris to Ursa Minor and Major
I still wore

it I'm sure. I can't recall every place
I've ever been to, *con perdón*, because
I am older than fiftythree million years,
but Percepta, you're clever, if you say so
I'll try:

I had it on Pegasus, Taurus, and Betelgeuse,
Serpens, Hydra, Canis, Monocerus,
Corona, Draco, Cassiopeia and Cygnus
north, south, east, west – wherever I flew
I had my shoe.

I wore it in Greenland, New York, the Sahara,
in Sydney, Rome, Cape Town and
    Connemara,

Moscow, Berlin, on the Hill of Tara,
on Lough Erne swanning round with cousin Fred
my foot never got wet.'

Percepta looked at the angel's face,
straight into his sad multi-coloured eyes,
then like lightning she ran upstairs
and in her hand when she came back
was a red sock

'*Mille gracie*,' said the angel slipping into it.
It's soft and warm and a perfect fit.
Auf Wiedersehn, this I will never forget.
One thing about angels — when we say never
it's for forever.'

He took a run, lifted off and started to fly.
His wings creaked, he was lop-sided and slow.
Percepta watched till he was a speck in the sky.
Her mother asked her later that night
why was she so quiet.

Next morning Percepta fed her dog Sam outside.
She spotted something silvery, soft and white
in the grass. The angel's shoe no doubt.
She picked it up — light as a feather —
and kept it forever.

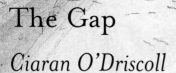

The Gap

Ciaran O'Driscoll

No need to get into a flap,
but when you take a nap —
Mind the Gap!
Be careful you don't drop through him
(or should I say 'through it'?)
into a bottomless pit.

And when you are awake
for heaven's sake
be sure you do not walk into his lair —
because that sneaky Gap hides everywhere.

Cracks in the pavement,
cracks in the wall —
no doubt the Gap is lurking in them all.
Look out, then, or you'll stumble in his trap.

He's also in the sky, that nasty Gap,
high up in a very ugly cloud,
waiting to open and let fall
an enormous hailstone ball
right on top of your head.

Good-bye.

Beware the Gap, he'd love to see you dead,
or at least more dead than alive.

So when you're taken for a drive,
don't forget to buckle down
your safety belt, in case
he has smuggled an empty space
into the floor below your feet
or the stuffing of the seat,
and plans to suck you in.

Very few adults know
about the Gap and his disasters;
only some railway station masters
have spotted how he crouches
between the platform's edge
and the doorstep of a carriage,
lying in wait for slouchers.

And that's why there are posters
in certain railway stations
that say Beware the Gap!
Attention: Mind the Gap!
But nobody takes any notice.

They think it's all a load of c··p,
until they're swallowed by the Gap.

Mal Magú

Biddy Jenkinson

Ba mhaith liom bheith im thaibhse mór:
ní bhactar riamh le taibhsín bídeach.
Dá mbeinn chomh mór le teach dhá stór,
ababú! Bheadh spórt is spraoi agam.

Chuirfinn eagla ar mo Mham,
is chrithfeadh Daid nuair a déarfainn 'Bú!'
Theithfeadh múinteoirí go beo
ón taibhse millteach, Mal Magú.

Ní osclóinn doras riamh arís.
Seo liom trín bhfalla, 'í-í-í!'
'Fág an áit! Glan as mo shlí!'
Magú, an taibhse, seachain í!

Thógfainn eilifint ón Zú
is rachainn ag marcaíocht air. Hurais!
Rithfeadh púcaí lenár dtaobh
is d'eitleodh feannóg inár ndiaidh.

Ní bheinn béasach. Ní bheinn ciallmhar.
Dhéanfainn ríl sa spéir, istoíche.
'Míle murdar,' déarfadh daoine,
'Sin í Mal, ar mhuin na gaoithe!'

Ligfinn 'í-á-ú' is míle.
Ní rachainn a luí go luath, choíche.
Aililiú! Dá mbeinn mór millteach!
Ochón! Mise Mal, taibhsín bídeach.

Song of Cuhtahlata, Lost Cherokee Mother

Ann Egan

Refrain:
For the wind was in my eyes, Little One,
the eastern reeds trilled in my ears,
the snow scaled my heart, Little One
'til I felt no fears, shed no tears.

I leave you my call from the wild, Little One,
medleys of rustles beneath the leaves.
I leave you my last handclasp in our canyon
where earth's music plays and heaves.

I leave you the beat of my pulse, Little One,
chant of beams while the moon weaves,
a fanfare of violas pitched deep in caves,
sound of woodwind that wanders and grieves.

I leave you the imprint of my palm, Little One,
your grip's hold and your lifeline's luck,
the ways of my days as they fretted full
of your cry's melody, your fingers' pluck.

I leave you the grief of my going, Little One,
I have borne you each moment in my heart.
I think of the songs you were singing,
all our lost lullabies, and we so far apart.

In the wisdom of our mountain, Little One,
I followed our people's trail and custom's scroll
bade us part with our elders, not our infants.
I broke the pattern of my soul.

For my love of the earth, Little One,
secrets and canons I held so dear,
I went from you to answer its call.
It scores my heart now like a spear.

At each day's rising, each night's falling,
in stretches of silence, flourishes of play,
you believed I was not with you,
Oh, Little One, I never left you, even for a day.

Refrain:
For the wind was in my eyes, Little One,
the eastern reeds trilled in my ears,
the snow scaled my heart, Little One
'til I felt no fears, shed no tears

[Note: Cuhtahlata is a girl's name of the Cherokee people. It means 'wild hemp'.]

89

Pangur Bán's Revenge

Iggy McGovern

Call me Pangur Bán; this cat
knows exactly where it's at.
Never mind my soppy name;
violence is my favourite game.

That's my Master large of girth,
copying for all he's worth,
thinks he's God's gift to the cat
corpulent upon the mat.

Would to God he'd get a life,
quit the Church and take a wife,
start to act like a real man,
take his cue from Pangur Bán.

Bad enough that he should be
fieldmouse of the monastery.
Now he treads on P.B.'s paw,
ptth, this is the final straw.

Yesterday, he would recite
lines he had been 'moved to write'.
Wonder where he gets these views?
Pangur Bán unlikely muse?

Mews, more like, as I complain
that my bowl is dry again;
fitting if his rheumy eyes
are the cause of his demise.

Up the staircase creep The Norse,
each as ugly as a horse.
Wholesale pillage is their plan
in the style of Pangur Bán.

Into the Scriptorium
bursts the cream of Nordic scum
Master snatches up his work,
starts to flee from the berserk,

heading for the secret door,
fails to notice on the floor
Viking raiders' biggest fan,
stretched-out form of Pangur Bán.

Master tumbles to the ground
masterpiece becomes unbound.
Master meets an awful fate
(one that I will not relate

it would only make you squirm)
Nor indeed will I confirm
rumours of a cat who sells
bits of the real Book of Kells!

If you're down by Botany Bay,
and you meet an old, white stray,
call him Pangur Bán: that cat
knows exactly where it's at.

Black Cat

Caitríona O'Reilly

Faint-hearted like any predator,
he plots massacres at the kitchen window
but is brainless at the fall of a leaf.
With such emphasis he arches his back,
quirked like my pinky from a cup,
an over-the-head cartoon question mark.
But for the oriental orbs of his eyes
(their pupils increasing like spills of ink),
he can abstract himself wholly, as though
done on a scroll in four swift strokes
to chase craneflies, insects written in grass.

Pearl and the Rhymes

Justin Quinn

There was a bunch of rhymes
out looking for a girl
to put her in a poem.
Along came one called Pearl.

The first rhyme said to her:

'You're such a dirty pup.
Come here, I'll clean you up
and scrape you with a comb
and put you in our poem.'

Pearl nearly ran away ...

But the next rhyme said to her:

'You don't look well to me.
I'll feed you broccoli
and carrots from our home.
You'll be fit for our poem.'

Pearl nearly ran away ...

But the next rhyme said to her:

'Your clothes are such a mess!
Put on this nice pink dress
with frilly bits like foam.
You'll look cute in our poem.'

Pearl nearly ran away ...

But the last rhyme said to her:

'No scraping with a comb.
No carrots from our home.
No frilly bits like foam.
For really it's your poem
where you can come and play
just as you are and stay
an hour or for a day.
Come on, what do you say?'

Pearl didn't run away.

A Keen for the Coins

Seamus Heaney

O henny penny! O horsed half-crown!
O florin salmon! O sixpence hound!
O woodcock! Piglets! Hare and bull!
O mint of field and flood, farewell!
Be Ireland's lost ark, gone to ground,
And where the rainbow ends, be found.

...something beginning

Mornsong

Dennis O'Driscoll

Rise in the morning,
face the unknown.
Iron your skin
and polish your bone.

Eat up your breakfast
of pie in the sky.
Your thoughts are the best
that pennies can buy.

Clouds are like dripping
stuck to a bowl.
Rain is a mare
giving birth to a foal.

It's time you left home
for the front of the class.
The wider the mark,
the greater the gas.

Your school is a lab
where test tubes play pranks.
Your class is a form
where you fill in your blanks.

Pack a lunch of smoked apples
or cornflakes and fries.
Splash out on fresh rainshine,
yawn open your eyes.

House Proud

Frank Ormsby

You'll like our porch.
To put you at your ease
our Laughing Buddha
chimes on every breeze.

Our lantern porchlight
joys in shadow-play.
Its daylight sensor
keeps the dark at bay.

Inside our walls are panelled.
The stained glass
on the landing
exudes a certain gravitas.

Christmas trees and luggage
take a year
out in our attic.
Dust loves to settle here.

Our conservatory hosts the sun.
Here even showers
are therapeutic.
At night the moon is ours.

On winter days
our heated kitchen floor
would tempt you to kick
your shoes off at the door.

Our north-facing garden
is the place to go
for snow and blackbirds —
in case you didn't know!

Nothing pretentious. We think
you'll share our view
that *tous le monde*
would feel at home *chez nous.*

Poem for a Baby

Desmond O'Grady

When you were born you came to us
with birth's first cry and laugh.
Your opened eyes blinked, curious
at your first sight of life.

Consumated mother, father
we praise your every pose.
Praying our love into your ear
We see you our love's prize.

We communion, confirm your life
with water, bread and wine.
That may postpone some human grief,
protect your family home.

In time you too will do the same
for yours when they are born.
That will renew, pass on your name
to your own grandchildren.

Bordeaux Macho

John Montague

Pierre, from next door,
swaggers to claim his girlfriend,
wrapped in a serape
made from a looped cloth,
with a revolver
stuck in his belt,
ordering, from all
his full seven years
of Southern manhood
to Sibyl, *Come here*.

She, a modern miss,
does not answer, or budge,
but serenely hands him a dish
to wash, and dry with his cloth.

On Water

John O'Donnell

I'd seen it happen years ago, back when
he was just a child; couldn't have been more
than eight. I'd warned him: stay close to the shore,
don't go deeper than your knees. But even then
he had this way of doing what he thought was right.
My back was turned — his baby sister, red-cheeked
in the heat — and he was gone. I panicked;
ran down to the edge, screamed his name in fright
until I saw him, going out with the tide
walking on water. Little splashes as
he skipped from wave to wave; astonished fishes
leaping out from underneath his feet. Arms stretched wide,
he smiled back, showing how easily it was done.
Which it was, compared with what was yet to come.

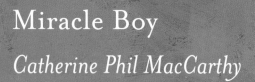

Miracle Boy

Catherine Phil MacCarthy

You learn tricks
on a new BMX,
wheelies
and bunny hops,

gain speed and loop
long back a hoop
against azure
birthday skies.

The weather pitch
half-laid is rich
as a cinder path,
terrain to pull

bars into the air
as if it were
your own element
and flight second nature.

You've taught me to see
you defy gravity,
speak the lingo
for where would life be

without rotations,
funky chickens,
infinity rolls?
Despite fear

of losing control,
falls and wipe-outs,
as you clear a ramp
or a half-pipe,

your passion sparks
taking risks,
wheels, wings
riding thermals

in an open sky,
like that boy
who ran free
of the labyrinth

and flew so high:
dare I pry —
of these cheats
of mortality,

this hunger
for eternity
amid all the buzz —
if you know Icarus?

103

Alpine Interlude

In memory of Miriam Aoife Agee, 1997-2001

Chris Agee

When we reached the mountain bog in the saddle
Of Jackson, and saw the heads of thousands
Of cotton sedge trembling and bobbing, letting go

Their fleecy tufts like thistledown in Ireland
Over archipelagos of blackbrown peat sediment —
I thought, after a while, of those days in Kosovo: life
Essential in its passing, its beauty, its tragedy. But first
Pausing long trail minutes, the boy becalmed on
Planks of bog bridge, seeing mountain cranberry,

Pale laurel, Canada mayflower, windy Appalachian bog
Rimmed by Labrador tea, the sweetness of the moment
Reminded me of Miriam's life, its brevity and softness,

Its summery interlude, its sunniness stretching
Out to the unending dark dwarf balsam fir-trees
And the great universe bowl of the White Mountains

In sheer airy blue outline, the cumuli sailing in
Puffs of snapdragon and Hiroshima ... with which,
Nonetheless, in the mind's eye, her time seemed one.

Script

Moya Cannon

The double line of prints
showed where a pup had dragged itself up
a few yards above the tidemark.
It panted, blinking away the driven sand,
while a wind-ripped tide ebbed fast.

A few other November strays
arrived to taste the end of the gale —
a couple in bright raincoats, down for the weekend,
and two boys on bikes who'd heard the news.

Rested now, maybe, or scared,
it took off down the long white beach,
its blubbery weight gallumphing
as it pulled itself up and forwards on its front flippers
building up speed
until its flesh rippled and it was carried
as much by rhythm as by strength,
like the great statues on Easter Island,
like ourselves.

It stopped, its sides heaving
as if the small grey-spotted body might burst
but gathered itself and set off again
collapsing again, yards short of the water, spent.

After a long time it raised its head,
hauled itself down the last slope of sand,
through the first thin broken waves,
into its own depth
and then nothing
but the winter sea
and the double row of prints.

We walked down the shore for a closer look.

Dug hard into the sand,
claw-marks
recorded a breast-stroke,
a perfect, cursive script
which reached
the ocean's lip.

Tree

Katie Donovan

I am out in the wind
and standing firm.

It's not like
being taken in
and showered
in silver.

Not like
being dressed in light,
my scent
lifting the room.

This is where
I don't have
to cut off
my roots.

Bee-chasing

Nessa O'Mahony

You stalk
eying montbretia flames
levelling ferns ...

now stock-still
tracking a bee's flight,
waiting for the exact point
in its trajectory
to pounce,

the learned grace
of an aerial acrobat
claws
arching
as you complete
a perfect somersault ...

and miss once more.

Outside
a car brakes;
ears flatten
as you arrow back
to safety.

Homework with Her Cat

Eamonn Wall

Slowly, she draws books from her lavender bag.
There's Science, Maths, *French: An Introduction*,

& *The Merchant of Venice*. Each is covered in brown
paper — her mother's touch — & slyly decorated with

leaves, hearts, and daffodils. From the front room,
she hears Dad snore to Anne Doyle on the Nine

O'Clock News. Though it's forbidden, she listens
to the radio through the headphones she has kept

hidden in her pencil case. Outside, through the
kitchen window, she sees rainwater's begun

to form in puddles under the yellow lights in front
of Susan O'Leary's house. She's mean, everyone

says of Susan, and she has a big nose. Country 'n'
Western: she turns off the radio, conceals her

headphones so that the wires wiggle in a bevy
of markers. Quickly, out of nowhere, Ghostie

lands on top of her pile of books and copies.
Purring already, and purring more when she pets

him under the chin, & even more so as she runs
the outside of her palm tailwards, along each bony

cheek. If white cats have matching eyes they
are blind, but Ghostie is not blind: he can spot

a robin from a mile away. When it comes to
education, this cat's on top of things. He's

stretched over knowledge as old as Ancient Greece,
as modern as the phrases used by the ultra cool

sophisticates of Gay Paree, nibbling croissants
in cafés along the Boulevard St. Germain. When

she tries to liberate Portia from under his front
paws, Ghostie leaps from the table scattering pens

and papers. After yelling his name too loudly, she
recalls what Mam says: 'Nora, be kind to your animals.

They will always be kinder to you than the boys
you'll meet.' Then, with her ruler, she roots hard

to rescue a red marker from under the cooker.
On all fours on the floor, Ghostie rubs against

her outstretched arm, gives cat kisses to her
nut brown hair. Once, in Confirmation class,

she announced that cats have souls and was
clipped across the ear by Sister Florence. Mam

says all animals, plants, and even insects have
souls and that that's what's called ecology, and

that ecology will save the world from ruination.
Order restored, she makes her Dad a cup of tea,

two slices of toast with marmalade, then wakes
him in time for *Questions & Answers*. With

Ghostie curled in Mam's chair beside the old
range, she flies through her exercises and her

many memorisations, and learns that at one
time they used ducats in Venice though they

spend euros now like the rest of us. She is
waiting on the doorbell. Mam's yellow fleece

& jet black hair proceeding quickly homeward
from her aerobics class in the Boys' Club Hall.

My Day

(MARCH 1845)

Máighréad Medbh

I sit up in our bed of straw and listen to the birds.
We're a wild bunch of bodies all the same –
straw over, straw under.
Mammy shuddered when I wondered
if we're kindred to the animals with no souls.
She crossed herself and Cathal frowned, and I stuttered to explain –
'We're in the same byre, walk the same miry floor,
we eat together, sleep together in our clothes.
The Connors children run out naked,
not just summer, winter too;
even them that's in the bigger places –
under gowns and mirrored faces –'
well I never finished out my say.
Cathal went, 'You'd better not,' and I was on my own again,
thinking things that turn me into something wrong.

There she's up and by the fire, like she always seems to be,
like an Israelite waiting for the word.
The boys are on their straw, Daddy's in the loft;
they're asleep but it's never silent here —
hoo and cluck and grunt and chew and the sounds that blow in to us,
people passing, children crying on the road.
With the slit of window light and the brightening of the turf,
I can see that she's looking at me straight.
She gives her Sunday of a smile —
you know I'd see that dark or bright —
and I make out what she's holding in her lap.
It's my only good bodice that I stitched up late last night,
so I'd cut a dash like any at the wake.
'Rena, girl,' she says, 'you're a fine young woman now.
I was thinking this must be your birthdate.'

She says I needn't wish for more than this —
the birds gone mad with spring,
potatoes in the pit,
myself pink and healthy and fourteen.
I get water from the well and look closely in the pail,
splash my face with my reflection, comb my hair.
I'll be watching for the man who'll know I understand,
who'll whisk me, like a story, far away —
a poet or professor or a travelling prince!
I'll be pretty, simply waiting for my day.

The Violet Maker

Medbh McGuckian

Steel dust, stone dust, clay dust, fibre dust,
breathed and breathed and breathed again.

Weekly, she has been growing thinner,
a well, fine, young, enamelled-ware brusher,
who never had a day's sickness.

She handles each flower four times,
five hundred and seventy-two handlings
for three farthings. And it may be
that her gums show a very faint blue line …

One morning, while brushing her hair,
she has lost all power in both of her wrists:
it deepens without warning into one half
of her face, then the arm and leg
on the same side of her body.

She requires to be roused,
when she is found wandering,
her pulse which was half-yellow, half-white,
is grey-green as March.

Yarn

Colette Nic Aodha

We cornered the flock
after racing around the paddock,
child-pens, we stood at set locations.
There was always a baa renegade,
black-faced and sure-footed.
We watched with awe as hooves were hooked,
bales of live wool, grounded.
Knee on belly, experts sheared,
almost avoided all flesh,
the odd bit of mutton
peeked out behind snowdrifts.
The folded woollen coats
were parcelled with oily yarn,
many were spun while Aed,
the one-eyed god, shone down.
That evening we went home,
packed some of the takings
into a canvass sack,
that drooped from our barn roof.
The rest was bussed off,
returned as Foxford blanket
or smelly yellow thread.
I stood, hands outstretched,
as it was unravelled and rewound,
shaped by maternal needles to *geansaí* or scarf.

In the Bakery

Gerard Smyth

I sliced the round fruit down to the core,
a tight knuckle that tasted sour.
Good hands lined with flour
were creating something beautiful
out of the dough, beating it flat.

'Silence Is Golden', someone sang on the old radio
that used to fade and then come back.
It was almost a biblical task —
taking from the oven the abundance
of the baker's dozen: soda farls, apple tarts,
wheaten bread with a crust of thickness.

It was a place of sifting fingers
and measuring vessels, of work
that became a ritual when I filled
and emptied the kiln
or gathered up egg shells and apple skins.

Slipstream

Maurice Harmon

Stuntman of the skies, formation flying
over the sea from Gormanstown, banking
into the sun, the mountains of Mourne turning
to roam the air with you, the great plain

levelling beyond Tara and the Boyne
to where, a sweet grape-blue, Dublin's hills
are delicately scrolled towards Rockabill.
What you really loved were solo flights.

You looped the loop so many times
the watching heads were swivelled into knots.
You calmly dived beneath the viaduct
and dropped your washing home at Lusk.

Each time I see dare-devils now,
tricked out in goggles, leather helmets, mitts,
I see you soaring, banking, dipping,
shutting the engine off, dropping into

free-fall, loving the sibilant rush
of air, the land flying beneath your feet,
a heart-stopping world in waiting;
then giving the engine a kiss of life,

tilting upward to cones of cloud, wind-whorled,
your thumb upstretched to mine, standing,
scared upon Ardgillan strand,
my hands miming airy turbulence.

Sculpture Yard, USA

Macdara Woods

Waking at five fifteen a.m.
in the dark
        With the rain
still keeping the pollen down –
damp and down since seven last night –
and a slow purposeful hoot
mournful and sombre
the organ note of a train
on the Norfolk Southern sounds
through the walls of the barn
fills up the space of my room
before passing on through the night
and the rain and dark and I wait
for sleep or the next one
waiting for now or for morning tomorrow
for breakfast and light
and the scarlet knowledge of cardinal birds:
to be safe in this white cell
listening to distance itself go by
these are momentous events
when nine short days
are longer than months – and a month
is as vast
as the beckoning mountains

The Sleeping Sailor

Matthew Sweeney

Under the upturned boat
lay a sailor.
He wasn't dead, only sleeping –
sleeping off a night of rum.
When he'd staggered back from the pub
it had been raining
so he'd turned over the boat
and climbed inside.
Out on the bay his ship waited.
Already the Captain paced his cabin,
muttering to the walls.
When the first rays of sunlight
sparkled on the bay –
and all the rain left the sky
and an early dog came sniffing,
then barking at the boat –
the sailor woke.
His head hurt.
His mouth was dry.
He cursed the dog,
heaved the boat right way up,
dragged it to the water,
gathered his oars
and began to row.
An eye at the end of a telescope
watched him approach,
and underneath it a grim smile grew.

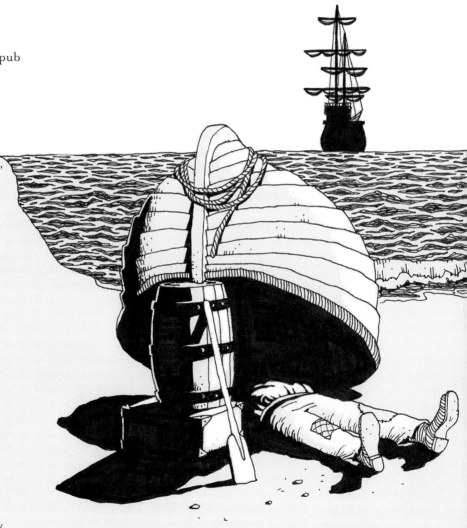

Instructions for Suburban Living

Al Reza

I woke up this Tuesday morning
and I felt so confused
I knew that I'd misplaced my
Instructions for Suburban Living.

Suddenly not a lot of things made se

I didn't want to queue
for my ticket at the train station.
I didn't want to go to work either
for that matter.

I couldn't see a pattern anymore.

My head was filled with strange ideas:
stop working
quit your job
stand on street corners
sell books
sell paintings.

And all the people rushing by
didn't seem happy
but at least they knew
where to go.

But just as I was giving up
standing there paralysed
I saw a seagull
reflected in a puddle.
It reminded me
to look up
now & again.

But no time to think
of such things.
I've got to go
got to keep moving
got to find my
Instructions for Suburban Living.

BELFAST
EXPRESS

118

Anto's Inferno

Rita Ann Higgins

It wasn't until our Anto
got fourteen months
for borrowing other people's cars
from their driveways
and making an inferno out of them
so that he could show his uncles
what a big man he was —
then and only then did we realise
what an insatiable appetite he had.

After he was lock-jawed
in The Joy for a few months
our house was like a banqueting hall
with all that extra food.
Going through that food
was like a journey through hell
heaven and purgatory.

Anto's friend, Liver Lips,
called round one day
to tell us one thing about Anto.
— I'll tell ya one thing about Anto,
he has great taste, he never touched nothin'
'cept Beamers and Mercs
and if they hadn't alloy wheels
there was no way he'd entertain them.
He'd babysit the odd Saab,
but only if she was a zero four job.

We miss Anto 'round the house;
only the other mornin'
before I did the shop
I opened our fridge —
there was enough frozen pizza in it
to feed all Castle Park,
untouched and no takers;
they were just sittin' there
like Beatrice, waitin' for the beck.

Hell

Adam Wyeth

It was hot as hell
that summer, so just for the hell
of it I ran away. Like mum, I traversed hell's
half acre and created hell.
I thought: Dad won't have a cat in hell's
chance of catching me, come hell
or high water I'll escape. But hell
for leather he found me. Hell's
bells, he yelled. What the hell's
your game? There'll be hell
to pay for you until hell
freezes over! And he did give me complete hell.
But he'd been so hell-
ish to mum I kept my hell-
acious self up. I was hell-
bent in galling him, so to play hell,
I pulled out his beloved hell-
eborine as soon as we got home. Of course all hell
broke loose. He said I was just like my hell-
cat mother, but I know he still loved her hell-
enic beauty deep down. Since she had left we had gone to hell
in a hand basket, he turned home into a total hell-

120

hole. I missed mum like hell,
thus I became the hell-
ion I was, descending rapidly on a hell-
ward course. There wasn't a hope in hell
for me. I didn't say hell-
o to anybody anymore. I became hell-
raiser as much as possible. Then like a bat out of hell
I absconded again, with some Hell's
Angels this time, we had a hell-
uva ride. Dad thought I was definitely in for hell-
fire, and I did go to hell
and back over everything. But I wasn't a real hell-
hound. Just like any rebel, I was confused as hell.

A Cigarette in an Ashtray

Matthew Geden

The bar-room clock hands have almost stopped
caught between tick and tock, those partners in
time. My life is in ashes. Wistfully I watch
my grey soul slipping guiltily out; going to join
the gathering clouds above. I have lain untouched

for some time, burning alone amongst the remains
of former friends. No hand reaches out for me.
Already I feel smaller, older and strangely
short of breath. I miss the ordinary:

the flourish in the air, the regular kiss
of warm puckered lips, the fire in my belly
and the smell of you. My only wish,

as I watch another cigarette being lit,
is that they find some cure for this ending of life.

Any minute now the bar-man will call, 'Time'.

Poisoned

John Ennis

All the late sunlit afternoon he lay, my brothers' collie
by the garden hedge, but out the south-facing riverfield side
his white teeth parted in little ivories for his tongue.
Glossy bluebottles circled his open almond eyes.

It must have been late August or so for the pippins
up in the old tall trees ripened red and unseen
the appled side of the hedge where the bitter crab grew.
His bushy tail was rigid and his thin legs were too.

Corn was on the noisy mind of everyone, it seems,
the tall barley bearding you like an older brother, then
oats, wheat as well in the golden sun. After supper, they'd bury him
sorrowing, one to the other, for he never bothered sheep.

And I who loved to reach up my two arms
to meet round his ruff neck, rub the slender nose that tapered
or touch the black-tipped ears that looked forward,
hurried on by in the hot sun for his flies lit on me
and I was so afraid in my heart of the dead.

Bully

Enda Wyley

You are a sharp pencil
in my side during every class,
a robber of all the homework I do,
a smiling, sweet face to the teacher
but a hissing, green-eyed demon to me.

You are cruel glass in the playground,
a towering wall that blocks my way home.
You push, kick, bruise, taunt, sneer, laugh
at me — there is nowhere you won't find me.
My nights and mornings have your cruel stare.

But there'll come a time when you'll fall down,
when you'll cry out, when you'll be left alone.
Then who will help you up, dry your eyes, brush
dust from your knees, gently wash your cuts clean?
Who will take your hand and walk home with you?

TXT—UR

Paula Meehan

Wots d crak? Its Mick frm d plex. Keiths m8.
In d park. Wanna stall it? Bring a cr8!

N me way. Is dat uzer fire B-side d g8?

N.e chance of hukn-up again? Last-nite woz gr8!

STOP THIS OBSCENITY AT ONCE. KATE'S

MAM HERE. I'LL CALL THE GUARDS. YOU REPROBATE!

U prik, im groundid. D lox r changed! Just u w8
til me Da gets iz handz n u! He'l b8

lumps outta u!
                          Lets start again. A cleen sl8.
Dnt wrk ureself up n2 such a st8!

Last of me cred! Rekn me hed! 2 much n me pl8.
Dnt even no if dis is luv r if dis is h8!

Dats cool chix, but dnt leev it 2 l8.
Deyre Q-ing up 4 me all over dis est8!!

His i's Were Empty

Rita Ann Higgins

The only thing I liked
about my father
was his handwriting.

His n's were slender and mean,
they had big city-never seen
written all over them.

His r's were turned in secret-keepers
they stole or owed nothing
to chance or design.

His n's were nowhere now
but they had travelled
through continents
of isolation and sting.

His m's were memorable,
his mother was free,
she died before she could
wing him a lullaby.
His m's now mine to take or leave
I took a left and lost.

The spines of his k's
were sentinel straight —
once teddy-boy wise
now corner-men lonely.
The watchers of history
the warmers of stone.

His g's were fractured and cross,
snarling like the Leitir Móir mongrels
at the cheating half-days of winter.

His eyes were empty,
except for that gulf of longing
that gaped around syllables,
making contact a cavity
language never reached.

In the Pressure Cooker

Ann Leahy

For milestones there were appliances
umbilically attached to the wall.
Like the polisher that, early on,
would circle like a dancer out of control,

spreading wax in scarified rings,
around downstairs rooms,
the house charged and tense
from its fulminating roars,

or the twin-tub that meant a day
of sudsy puddles out the back
eventually breaking down
to make way for an automatic:

nine programmes, pre-rinse and spin.
One tight cube that took everything in
and drew no attention to itself
like well behaved children.

When the pressure cooker
came its manual
was read and read again,
its first spin and hiss a thrill;

everyone gathered round as if
to watch some young hopeful
perform. And the same fear —
that it might not settle

to a controlled release
of steam. Explode instead,
spray us all with shrapnel
from its stainless steel lid.

The kitchen became
a fluorescent-bulb shrine,
where Krupps motors droned
beneath a steamy benediction,

those metallic pressure-cooked
stews — our staple. As long,
that is, as we could keep
the lid screwed down.

Oops

AFTER FREUD

Gerry Murphy

The old woman
so small that, when I held
the shop door open for her,
she passed in easily
under my arm.
Somewhere in that split-second
between the chivalrous act
and the thought
that the ungrateful cow
might be treating me
as a doorman,
I released the heavy,
tightly-sprung door.

I still hear the thump
as it caught her
in the small of her back.

Oidhreacht

Áine Ní Ghlinn

Tusa a chabhraigh liom
na huibheacha a chomhaireamh
sa nead spideoige a bhí folaithe
ag an eidhneán ag bun an ghairdín.

Tusa a bhain an leabhar mór anuas ón seilf
a chuaigh tríd leathanach ar leathanach
nó go bhfacamar
uibheacha ár spideoige.

Tusa a rinne roicéad liom
as cathaoir chistine
is a bhí mar chomhphíolóta agam
ar ár gcéad thuras go Mars.

Tusa a chaith na laethanta fada liom
ag faire ar na damháin alla is na péisteanna
a shiúil abhaile liom faoi ualach duilleogach
ár bpócaí ag cur thar maoil le hiontaisí na coille.

Tusa an té a raibh an t-am agat
is a roinn an t-am sin liomsa.
Anois agus tearmann do láimhe móiré imithe uaim
beidh oidhreacht do chuid ama agam go deo.

I'm Not Stupid

Moyra Donaldson

Shouting rises
above the sound of the TV,
up through the ceiling, seeping
between the floorboards of my room
until I put my headphones on and tune it out,
get homework done, despite my parents arguing.

Tomorrow they'll
pretend it's all ok, tell me
there's nothing to worry about,
as if I'm just a kid and don't know
what's happening, mum's eyes all red from crying,
dad not talking and drinking too much and maybe leaving.

Do they think I'm stupid? That I don't know what's going on?

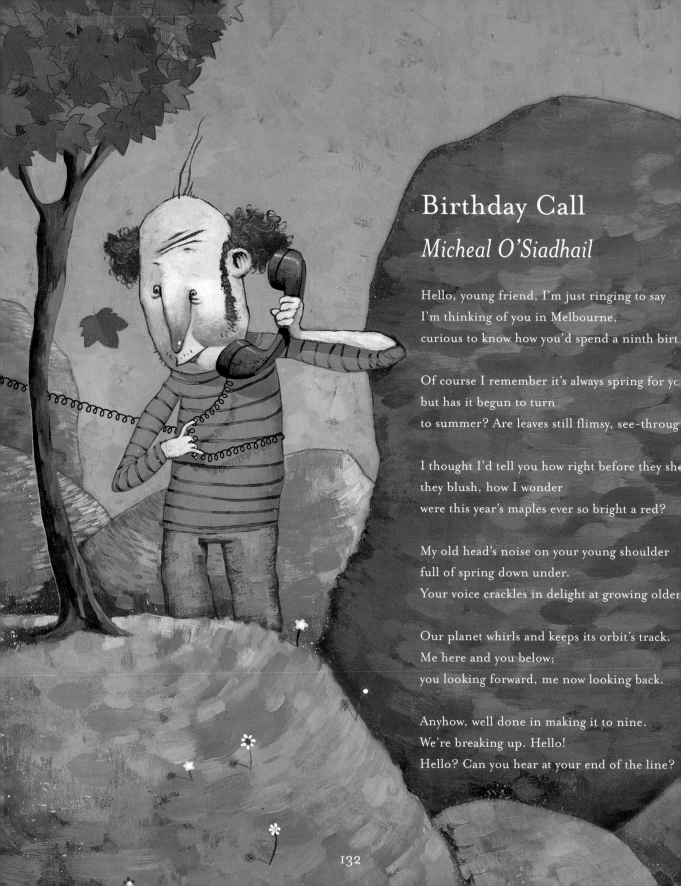

Birthday Call

Micheal O'Siadhail

Hello, young friend, I'm just ringing to say
I'm thinking of you in Melbourne,
curious to know how you'd spend a ninth birth

Of course I remember it's always spring for yc
but has it begun to turn
to summer? Are leaves still flimsy, see-throug

I thought I'd tell you how right before they sh
they blush, how I wonder
were this year's maples ever so bright a red?

My old head's noise on your young shoulder
full of spring down under.
Your voice crackles in delight at growing older

Our planet whirls and keeps its orbit's track.
Me here and you below;
you looking forward, me now looking back.

Anyhow, well done in making it to nine.
We're breaking up. Hello!
Hello? Can you hear at your end of the line?

My Family,
When I'm Angry

Jo Slade

My silly sister squabble sings,
'If I were a blackbird I'd whistle and sing …'

If I were a blackbird I'd be out of here.
I'd be the only bird on the wing –
a lone migrator to an unknown land
not mapped, never seen, an island for
the dropped in and leaving soon.
No gods, saints, mystics, angels,
wise old crabs, archetypes, visionaries,
no next of kin, kind old gran, friend of the family.
No one I know or have ever seen.

Nope, I'll jump ship, drown
I just won't hang around.
I won't *'Polly put the kettle on'*.
I'll hide – be a wheel in the garden
an oil tank overgrown with leaves,
I'll tell the cops I live with thieves.

Higgledy, piggledy, powder and gun
hide in the dustbin or they'll kill you for fun.

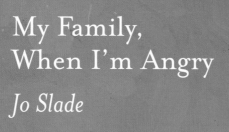

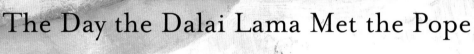

The Day the Dalai Lama Met the Pope

Sydney Bernard Smith

In the cold Tibetan highlands, in the panting heart of Rome
two mutually exclusive gods have found themselves a home;
for east was east and west was west until the horoscope
ordained the day the Dalai Lama went to meet the Pope.

Thought Chairman Mao: 'I wonder how their doctrines will agree —
of course there is no god — and if there was it would be me;
these religions must be desperate, but we'll give them lots of scope
and we yet may live to see the Dalai Lama hang the Pope.'

The two eternal travellers converse, each on his throne:
'Your Holiness feels well today?' 'Fine thank you, how's Your Own?
I fear our worlds are teetering on the verge of a perilous slope
— should we consider merging, Dalai Lama?' asks the Pope.

O come all ye true-born Orangemen, and admire the happy song
of two contraries reconciled, both right and neither wrong;
which shows beggars can be choosers, and unlikely pairs elope
— and where would the Dalai Lama be if Paisley met the Pope?

School Yearbook

Louise C Callaghan

I keep turning to his photo, the posed
face of my sister. A boy-soldier
home on leave, his last look.
The story goes of him arrested,
held over Easter in the Four Courts.
Ice winds ploughing up the Liffey.
Insurgents, young as himself
among the ruins, crouched in doors.
Any one of them could be
from his class in school.
The contradictory clatter of our war
sounding off the cobbled quay.

The Game

Fred Johnston

Sometimes it happened that you'd score a goal,
then you'd get the cheer and slap on the back.
Other times you'd miss or lose the ball or stumble
your best mates called you 'Stupid Fenian'
and you'd smile as a fist landed on your back.

You worked harder than the rest to find the wood
or tyres or bits of hedge and dried-up branches –
Bonfire Night arrived and you were out like a linty
feeling the boney heat like a slap in the lug,
reddening your cheeks as you fed it more branches.

You played the game and knew its every move,
half a child yet and wiser than your years:
Streets not to walk up alone, corners to avoid,
still these half-mates stood by you in any foreign scrap,
proudly *their* Fenian only, you'd remember that for years.

Dán do Theifigh

Micheál Ó Conghaile

Ba dhaoine deasa sinn, dúirt siad
fáilteach, gnaíúil gealgháireach
a d'fháiltigh ariamh thar muir isteach
roimh Fhrancach, Yank is Spáinneach.

Ba dhaoine deasa sinn, dúirt siad
ar chnoic ghlasa Éireann, faoi léigear sáile
a d'fhair amach don allúrach
ba ghile cneas is pócaí teannta.

Ba dhaoine deasa sinn, chreid siad
nach gcuirfeadh an dubh ar an mbán duit
ach conas is féidir an deas a mheas
nó go bhfaigheann seans bheith gránna.

The Human Zoo

Gerald Dawe

Sometimes I think of the night safe
at the bottom of our street.

I could be coming home from work
on a normal day in the middle of the week.

Before I know it I think of the night safe
locked in its stone and steel with the sign

in capitals overhead, NIGHT SAFE,
the bank closed, the blinds half drawn,

the lights on dim and an arrow that shows
a green man getting the hell out of there.

It can also be the other way around.
Once I saw an elephant taking a stroll

with its circus-minder and a couple
of tigers stretch out in their cages

and a llama stop in its tracks
to watch us, all seated, flying past,

but such things rarely last.

Leaving for a Nursing Home

Pádraig J Daly

She reaches a thin hand
to clutch at mine:
She is frail and frightened.

She must leave all that years
have made familiar
and go where she will lie at night

listening to the moans of strangers.
No more dusting jugs and photographs,
setting out cups,

filling at evening her hot water jar,
putting the door on double lock,
climbing the short stairs to her bedroom.

If a clock ticks, it will not be hers.
If a phone rings in the night,
it will be for some other.

Amen Woman

Noel Monahan

She was in love with colours,
streaks in her hair,
peacock feathers grew in her hat.
November winds danced on her summer dress
and she always said: *Amen, Amen.*

She pushed a wheelbarrow full of gadgets
through the streets,
shouting: lamp shades – clothes pegs – sun glasses –
nibs for pens – bottles for rheumatism;
and finally she would say: *Amen, Amen.*

She could call at any time
of day or night, front door, back door.
The cat kept a nervous eye on her,
the dog barked furiously
and she calmed him with her *Amen, Amen.*

She told us all the news,
who was getting married – what happened to Eileen
and more if you listened –
about Ukulele Joe and his midnight parties
and then she'd say, *Amen, Amen,* and trundle away.

She got lost somewhere
disappeared in the fog –
someone said she went to a brother in America,
others say she was old enough to die,
grew wings and flew to heaven, *Amen, Amen.*

Blue Willow

Mary O'Malley

By the moongate in Denis's garden
there's a pond. Shoals of tangerine fishes
blow bubbly kisses. A young pearl fisher
dives in to pick them. They turn to moon opals
a necklace of wishes for his princess.

Over there under the monkey-puzzle tree
there's a unicorn, sitting pretty
exactly like the famous tapestry in France
he has his silly eye on you but don't worry
he's a bit of a prancy dancer.

Now your tiger with his stripes on fire is rippling
through the moongate in Denis's garden.
Cool cool fiery cat, close your eyes and fancy that
by the silvery zip-zapping scissory rip-rapping
only pretending-to-sleep napping sea.

Riverdown

John F Deane

… Comes dribbling out of high peatlands,
innocent places, shriven, out of
marshy hollows, silent humplands where
mist-clouds shift and darken; from under

heather hemp-roots and moss-whorls
the secret tracks of foxes and the
rending places of the hooded crow;
gathering, down towards the white-washed

gable-ends of outhouses, grows
a stream. With eels like molten butter and
backs the colour of peat, their bellies
a softened gold, they shiver under low banks

by half-buried stones where drips of rain
plop-plappp off the couch grass …

… Come in now under this bridge and crouch,
child-small, the water gravelling shallowly;
touch the flake and moisture of the masonry,
inhabit for a while a tiny

nowhere, be lonely, stone, be fluid;
sometimes a car will pass above you,
the world will shudder and unnatural
ripples rake the water; only attend,

fall to absence, be unseeing, all
listening; somewhere close a wren jitters,
perhaps a skald from the upper fields
offers its harsh-pitched groan; you could be

child forever, a washed-down tree-root,
perfect, useless, desire stilled ...

... Stood, often, on bridges, watching down
and dropped something, twig or leaf
and ran, watched it show on the other
side — and gloated as if a victory

had been won; time it takes to run from
arch to arch, from twig to schooner, for
the child to fall to unbelief; water
runs out gold over smoother time-stones

in pools; sounds come human, the flat-lands
reached, where dullness stretches out
towards sea; in a curve the water deepens
to a pond, surface-still and dangerous,

the first dark holding; in the distance
the monastery bell calls noon,

... angel mystery, pause, to touch
earth, and turn again, as if something
has been declared; now you can drop your
home-made hook, worm impaled, the cork

focussing the louring afternoon; all
the rivers of the world flow down
into the sea and the sea won't
overflow; the trout, thumb-small,

feed on oozings from the mountain; brown
furzelands, bog-iris, rushes thriving
on marsh acres, stream fattening to river,
here and there a donkey brays or

cows plash into muddying water;
drag forward, restless, the hope always

for that one trout, throbbing and fleshfull,
that nervous kill, till dogs bark and you
climb barbed wire into someone's meadow;
sorrow now that your pilgrimage down

from high places has wearied you.
The pleasure is the travelling, see how tide
reaches here, how marshland melts to slob.
Stench of decay, mud-bubbles, mullet

sluppering in the shallows, gulls
raucous by the pier's excesses and your spring
has disappeared into sea-rot. Knowledgeable,
   something
achieved, gather yourself still for the endeavour,

hold onto longing for the one
centre, the life-force, home, the mystery ...

Night

Greg Delanty

Waking, the sky clear, only a few grey wisps
  of cloud in the firmament,
the only hint that the avuncular god of night
  was here, puffing away
on his spittly pipe, all reverie I imagine,
  feet up, comfy, at ease
at last, watching over us, not wanting to wake us,
  his poor clay charges, too early, slipping
away on soft falling moccasins of light.

Suddenly Autumn

Ulick O'Connor

It is heartening as the leaves brown,
to see the pert blackberry look down
tart to the tongue with bright gleam.
But today fear crackled off the crop
time has telescoped to make it seem
a day since Fall last fired the trees' top.

In the Desert

Eiléan Ní Chuilleanáin

Almost day, looking down
from my high tower in the desert:
the sandstorm blows up
cuts my tower in half:
a crooked scarf of sand
as high as the window
that looks towards the mountains.
I cover my eyes
with my red scarf that slants
wrapping my body
and when it is over
I look towards the desert
and I see him again
in the daybreak light
still walking nearer —
he must be half-blinded.

In the desert walking
I see them by the shining,
reflection of dawn light,
something bright sewn in the cloth
worn on the head
masking the face.
I see them glinting.

He is sand brown,
his clothes brown like sand.
Now he is closer,
I see his shadow
as the dawn rises,
a bending shadow
and he approaches the well
in the shade of the palm trees.

Coming to the well he lifts
its wooden covering. Night
and coolness are still down there.
The snakes lie in the well, males
and females coiled together, wet.
Before he dips his cup to drink
he salutes them saying, happy
snakes, like the poor people,
who have only the comfort men
and women find in each other.
Let me fill my cup, let me rest
here in the shadow.

I hear him praying, I see him drink.
He lies down in the shadow.
When will somebody come and release me
from the sand-frayed tower, from the red scarf
that covers me like a flame?

Medley for Morin Khur

Paul Muldoon

The sound box is made of a horse's head.
The resonator is horse skin.
The strings and bow are of horsehair.

II

The Morin Khur is the thoroughbred
of Mongolian violins.
Its call is the call of the stallion to the mare.

III

A call which may no more be gainsaid
than that of jinn to jinn
through jasmine-weighted air.

IV

A call that may no more be gainsaid
than that of blood kin to kin
through a body-strewn central square.

V

A square in which they'll heap the horse heads
by the heaps of horse skin
and the heaps of horsehair.

Jim-fish

Paul Murray

jim-fish

banished from the throne
of unimportant neptune
suddenly

peered over midnight
stone and saw
ten thousand

golden salmon rise
with yellow wings through
subterranean splendour

jim-fish happy
to be king-shell
coral wise

among the listening
importance of shell-folk
suddenly

was singing
for the shells' delight
dark primitives

of poetry

P is for Poetry

Tony Curtis

Today, P is for poetry.
Yesterday, P was for pirates:
perilous plunderers with
parrots and pieces-of-eight.

     P is not perfect like U or I
     but it's popular
     and looks like a lollipop,
     which is popular too.

You could bring P home.
Your Mum would say
P is pleasant and polite,
it always minds its P's and Q's.

     For Dad, P is everything
     that interests him:
     papers, politics, pints;
     there's even a P in sport.

When Granny visits,
P is for kisses:
she calls them pecks,
but I know they're kisses.

     For Grandad on his bicycle,
     P is for pedals,
     punctures, pumps,
     puffing and panting.

For sisters who think they're
ballerinas, P is for pirouettes.
For brothers, P is all about
penalties and perfect pitches.

At the zoo, P is the
prowling and purring
of panthers, who,
if they were allowed,

would eat my favourites,
the black and white pandas.
P is even the shape
of the giraffe's neck.

At the North Pole,
P is for polar bears,
and Pooh Bear who went
there in search of the pole.

On Saint Patrick's Day,
P is for parade.
At Christmas, P is for
presents and pantos.

The night before my exams,
P is for panic.
And one Tuesday each year,
P is for pancake.

In fairy stories,
P is the prince who
turned into a frog,
or the beautiful princess

who could feel the pea
under her posterior.
There's also the Pied Piper,
Puss in Boots and Harry Potter.

For writers, P is for pens.
For poor writers, P is for pencils.
For magicians, P is the poof
that makes things vanish.

For disgusting people,
P is for pickers:
nose-pickers, ear-pickers,
toe-pickers.

On Sunday, P is for prayer.
On Saturday, P is for play:
playground if it's pleasant,
playstation if it's pouring.

The number of words
beginning with
the letter P is
phantasmagorical.

But today, P is for poetry,
that odd little world
where you count the lines
and everything rhymes.

Everything rhymes!
I knew there was something
I forgot. O well, I suppose
it's just back to the start . . .

I'm off

TRANSLATIONS

I am very grateful to Diarmuid Ó Cathasaigh and to individual poets for assistance in preparing (and in some instances for providing) these prose translation guides for non-Irish speaking readers. Any errors in these texts are mine. *Editor.*

[17] Máire Mhac an tSaoi: *What are we doing yesterday, Granda?' a nonsense rime*
'Tell me a story, Granda.' 'A story, a story, a tail on the bird, a lame yellow mare, a foal since she is it. Liam and his son bleached on a stone / a fox minding sheep, O for the ram! O for the ram! O for the ram! a fox minding sheep, O for the ram!' 'What are we doing yesterday, Granda?' 'The same as we did tomorrow, children!'

[23] Nuala Ní Dhomhnaill: *Sruthán sa tSeapáin / A Stream in Japan*
Down at the bottom of the water swims the 'ayu' fish briskly on the river bed. 'Ayu, ayu' we shout happily when we see them. 'Ayu, ayu' we smack our lips tastily when we eat them.

[25] Úna Leavy: *Sa Bhaile / At Home*
There's no fireside like your own fireside. Hang up your coat, take off your shoes, get a cup of tea and sit by the fire. The curtains drawn, the old clock ticking, wind in the chimney whispering in the silence. The cat and the dog both asleep. There is no fireside like your own.

[26] Mícheál Ó Ruairc: *Ar an Seilf sa Leabharlann / On the Shelf in the Library*
Were you ever there on the shelf in the library? *[this refrain 'on the shelf in the library' repeats after each line].* There is sport and fun there. There is a man who travelled the world there. A fox and a brown rabbit live there. A poet is imprisoned there. There is war and famine there. There is history and geography there. There is love and heartbreak there. There are cops and robbers there. There's a cowboy on a horse there. There is trouble and suffering there. There's a fish from the riverbed there. There is a two-headed monster there. There is a Russian spy there. There is a ghost in hiding there. There is a witch on a broomstick there. The wonders of the world are there. Would you like to live there, on the shelf in the library?

[37] Celia de Fréine: *Síofra Sí / Síofra the Fairy*
Síofra Sí the tooth fairy works every night flying fast from house to house, collecting teeth carefully, lodging money under pillows, bestowing happiness every time, hurrying home at break of day, looking forward to her cup of tea.

[49] Gabriel Fitzmaurice: *An t-Amhránaí / The Singer*
The song opens out from the centre of my heart – I am the song here, I am the singer. I sing my hope, I sing my love, I sing my light, I sing my trouble. In the corner of a pub on my own, back to the wall, instead of being a popstar in Theatre, Park or Hall, in the corner of a pub singing for just myself, I am the singer here, I am the song.

[55] Áine Ní Ghlinn: *Bunoscionn / Topsy Turvey*
An ear dropped out of the sky and stood in the middle of the garden listening to the various noises all around – the purring of the cat, the roar of the river, the rustling of the leaves, the whisper of the trees, the barking of the dog, the whistling of the wind, the crying of the baby, the cawing of a crow, the whine of the swing, the creaking of the gate and the drone of a plane high above.

The ear curled and twirled and there was a strange sound as though all the noises of the garden were being swirled around. With that the ear disappeared on a gust of wind leaving a strange medley of sounds. The dog roared, the swing cried, the cat whistled, the gate barked, the river creaked, the baby droned. The trees purred, the wind cawed, a crow rustled and an aeroplane whined. The poet looked up. The ear was well gone but from somewhere up above there came a hollow, mocking laugh.

[72] Rody Gorman: *Ceist / A Question*
Yes, a question for you, O thrush [my love]: when you sing forth that tune early in the morning, are you communing [speaking] in the way your sort always do, or focussing your song intentionally on me?

[72] Tom Mac Intyre: *An Bhóín Dé / The Ladybird*
You show yourself – healer and store of wisdom [expert] – in the centre of the white page. I left you in my garden and, timid by nature, I forgot about you, my love, until my eyes closed last night: and there you were, back, alive and well, enframed in bright dreams, nymph of the woods, and jewel.

[88] Biddy Jenkinson: *Mal Magú (not translated).*

[130] Áine Ní Ghlinn: *Oidhreacht / Legacy*
You were the one who helped me count the eggs in the robin's nest we found hidden in the ivy at the foot of the garden. You were the one who took the book down from the shelf and went through it page by page until we found our robin's eggs. You were the one who helped me make a rocket from a kitchen chair, my co-pilot on our first trip to Mars. You were the one who spent long days with me watching spiders and worms, walking home laden down with leaves, our pockets overflowing with the wonders of the wood. You were the one who had time and who shared that time with me. And although the sanctuary of your big hand is gone the legacy of that time will stay with me forever.

[137] Mícheál Ó Conghaile: *Dán do Theifigh / A Poem for Refugees*
We were nice people, they said, welcoming, decent, cheerful, who bade welcome to those from overseas, the Frenchman, the Yank and the Spaniard. We were nice people, they said, on the green hills of Ireland, besieged by the sea on the lookout for the foreigner who was pale-skinned and with bulging pockets. We were nice people, they believed, who wouldn't try to hoodwink you. But how can you know what nice means, until it gets a chance to be mean?

BIOGRAPHIES

The Illustrators

Corrina Askin graduated in 1993 with an MA in animation. She has undertaken commissions for Channel 4, The Irish Film board/RTE, MTV, and S4C. In addition to book illustration work for Irish, UK and US publishers, she is also a printmaker and shows in various Dublin galleries. Her work is in public and private collections including the Mater Hospital and the House of Lords. She won a Bisto Merit Award for illustration of this book.

Emma Byrne, born in Wexford, is a painter and graphic designer. Her paintings have been exhibited in Ireland, the UK, Liechtenstein and Germany. She studied graphic design at Limerick College of Art and Central Saint Martin's College of Art and Design, London. She is currently designer with The O'Brien Press, and she art-directed this book. She won a Bisto Merit Award for illustration of this book.

Alan Clarke, born 1976, studied architecture in Dublin before switching to study illustration at Falmouth College of Arts. He has completed numerous commissions in Ireland and abroad, including children's books, murals, conceptual design work for animation and TV, book covers and political caricatures. He has exhibited in Ireland, the USA and Japan, and at the International Children's Book Fair in Bologna, Italy. He won a Bisto Merit Award for his illustration of this book.

The Poets

Chris Agee was born in San Francisco in 1956 and studied at Harvard University. In Ireland since 1979, he edits the journal *Irish Pages* and reviews for *The Irish Times*. He is author of two collections, *In the New Hampshire Woods*(1992) and *First Light*(2003) and due in 2008 is a third volume, *Next to Nothing*. He lives in Belfast.

Sara Berkeley was born in Dublin and now lives in San Francisco. Her *Facts About Water, New and Selected Poems* was published in 1994. She has also published a volume of short stories and a novel, *Shadowing Hannah* (1999).

Dermot Bolger, born in Dublin in 1959, is a poet, novelist and playwright. His novels include *The Journey Home* and *The Family on Paradise Pier*. His plays have received the Samuel Beckett Prize and other awards. He rarely leaves Dublin, for fear of being trampled by stray rhinos, and still doesn't eat his greens.

Margot Bosonnet started writing when her children had grown up. She is author of *Skyscraper Ted and other Zany Verse*, *The Scrabblemongers* and the wonderful *Red Belly* novels trilogy. She works in Trinity College Library and lives in Malahide.

Eva Bourke, a native of Germany, has lived in Ireland for most of her life. She has five poetry collections, most recently *Latitude of Naples* (2005), and has edited contemporary Irish poetry in German editions. She lives in Galway and is a member of Aosdána.

Louise C. Callaghan was born in Dublin and educated at UCD. She has travelled widely. *The Puzzle-Heart* is her first collection of poetry. She received an MLit in Creative Writing (in poetry) from St Andrew's in Scotland in 2007.

Dublin-born Siobhan Campbell's collections include *The Permanent Wave* and *The Cold That Burns*. An award-winner in the National Poetry Competition and the Troubadour Poetry Prize, she is a former director of Wolfhound Press and currently Course Director of the Creative Writing MA at Kingston University London and Publisher at Kingston University Press.

Moya Cannon was born in Dunfanaghy, Co Donegal in 1956 and now lives in Galway. Her new & selected poems, *Carrying the Songs*, was published in 2007. She has been an editor of *Poetry Ireland Review* and writer-in-residence in Ontario and at the Centre Culturel Irlandais, Paris. A recipient of the Brendan Behan and the O'Shaughnessy awards, she is a member of Aosdána.

Philip Casey, poet and novelist, was born in London in 1950 and grew up in Co Wexford. His collections include *The Year of the Knife: Poems 1980-1990*, (1991) and *Dialogue in Fading Light: New and Selected Poems* (2005). Novels include *The Fisher Child*, (2001) and *The Fabulists* (1994) which won the Listowel Writers' Week Novel of the Year. He established and maintains the 'Irish Writers Online' and 'A Guide to Irish Culture' websites. A member of Aosdána, he lives in Dublin.

Patrick Chapman was born in 1968. His four poetry collections include *The New Pornography* (1996), and *Breaking Hearts and Traffic Lights* (2007). He has also written short stories, *The Wow Signal* (2007) and an award-winning film, *Burning the Bed* (2003). He won first prize, story category, in the 2003 Cinescape Genre Literary Awards.

Sean Clarkin was born in New Ross, Co Wexford in 1941. He was the inaugural winner of the Patrick Kavanagh Award in 1971, and his collection *Without Frenzy* was published in 1974. He lives in Co Wexford.

Susan Connolly was born in Drogheda, Co Louth in 1956 where she now lives. Her first collection was *For the Stranger* (1993). She co-authored *Stone and Tree Sheltering Water*. She received the Kavanagh Fellowship in Poetry in 2001.

Patrick Cotter was born in Cork in 1963 where he still lives and works as Director of the Munster Literature Centre. His latest collection of poetry is *Perplexed Skin* (2008).

Tony Curtis was born in Dublin in 1955. He is the author of six collections, including *The Well in the Rain: New & Selected Poems* (2006). His work is also in a US volume *Days Like These: Three Irish Poets* (2007). He is working on an A to Z of Poems for Children. A recipient of The National Poetry Prize, he is a member of Aosdána.

PJ Daly was born in Dungarvan, Co Waterford in 1943 and now works as an Augustinian priest in Dublin. He has published several poetry collections including *Poems: Selected and New* (1988), and a collection translated into Italian has been published in Rome.

Gerald Dawe was born in Belfast in 1952. He has published six poetry collections, including *The Morning Train* (1999) and *Lake Geneva* (2003). He teaches at Trinity College Dublin.

Celia de Fréine writes in Irish and in English. A recipient of the Kavanagh Award and Gradam Litríochta Chló Iar-Chonnachta, her most recent collection is *Scarecrows at Newtownards*(2005). Her film-poem, *Lorg*, premiered during Imram 2007. She lives in Dublin and Connemara.

John F. Deane was born in Achill Island in 1943 and now lives in Dublin. His published work includes *Manhandling the Deity* and *The Instruments of Art*. He has many European citations and awards for poetry and translation. Also a novelist (*Undertow*, 2002) and short story writer, he founded Poetry Ireland, and The Dedalus Press (1985). He is a member of Aosdána.

Patrick Deeley is from Loughrea, Co Galway. His children's books include *The Lost Orchard* (won the Eilis Dillon Memorial Award), *My Dog Lively* and *Snobby Cat*. Poetry collections include *Turane: The Hidden Village* (1995) and *Decoding Samara* (2000). He is principal of a primary school in Dublin.

Greg Delanty (born, Cork 1958), teaches at St Michael's College, Vermont and but returns every year to his Kerry home. His *Collected Poems 1986-2006* was published in 2007. Other collections include *The Ship of Birth* (2003) and *The Blind Stitch* (2001). He has received a Guggenheim award for poetry.

Moyra Donaldson was born in Co Down in 1956. She has won the Allingham Award, and the Belfast 2001 Year of the Artist Award. She also writes for stage and screen. Poetry collections include *Snakeskin Stilettos* (1998), *Beneath the Ice* (2001) and *The Horse's Nest* (2006).

Katie Donovan, born in 1962, spent her youth on a farm near Camolin in Co Wexford. She is author of *Irish Women Writers: Marginalised by Whom?* (1988) and a co-editor of *Ireland's Women, Writings Past and Present* (1994) and *Dublines* (1995). Her poetry includes *Entering the Mare* (1997) and *Day of the Dead* (2002). She lives in Co Dublin.

Ann Egan was born in 1948 in Co Laois. Her awards include Listowel Writers' Week prizes, the Athlone Poetry Prize and the Oki Prize. Her first collection was *Landing the Sea* (2003). She also has a novel, *Brigit of Kildare* (2001). She lives in Co Kildare.

Desmond Egan, born in Athlone, Co Westmeath in 1936, founded The Goldsmith Press in 1972. He has nineteen collections of poetry, one of prose and two of translations of Greek drama. He is widely published in translation (18 collections). Awards include: National Poetry Foundation, USA (1983) and awards from Bologna , Macedonia (2004), and France (2005). A DVD and studies on his work have been published in the US. He lives in Co Kildare.

John Ennis was born in Westmeath in 1944. *Telling the Bees* (1995), *Selected Poems* (1996), *Tráithníní* (2000), *Near St. Mullins* (2002) and *Goldcrest Falling* (2007) are among his fourteen poetry collections. He co-edited *The Echoing Years: Contemporary Poetry and Translation from Canada and Ireland* (2006). He received the Kavanagh and Irish American Cultural Institute poetry awards. He is head of the School of Humanities at the Waterford Institute of Technology.

Peter Fallon established The Gallery Press in 1970 at the age of 18 and has edited and published more than 400 books of poems and plays. His own poetry collections include *News of the World: Selected and New Poems* (1998), *The Georgics of Virgil* (2004) and *The Company of Horses* (2007). He is a member of Aosdána.

Gabriel Fitzmaurice from Moyvane, Co Kerry, is author of over 40 books of poetry, ballads, essays and translations. Reviewing *The Wrenboy's Carnival* (1999) the US Booklist described him as 'the best contemporary, traditional, popular poet in English'. He co-edited *An Chrann Faoi Bhláth* (1991) and edited *Irish Poetry Now: Other Voices* (1993). His translations are collected in *Poems from the Irish* (2004). He has published several verse collections for children.

Matthew Geden was born in the UK and lives in Kinsale where he works as poet, translator and publisher. His published work includes *Kinsale Poems* and *Autumn: Twenty Poems by Guillaume Apollinaire* (2003).

Rody Gorman, born in Dublin in 1960, now lives in the Isle of Skye. His work includes *Fax and Other Poems* (1996), *Cùis-Ghaoil* (1999) and *Naomhóga na Laoi* – a 2003 collection in Irish, Scottish Gaelic and English. He has been a Writer Fellow at UCC and in Skye, and is editor of *An Guth*.

Mark Granier, born in London in 1957, has lived in Dublin since the early 1960s. He has two collections: *Airborne* (2001) and *The Sky Road* (2007). Awards include The Vincent Buckley Prize in 2004.

Vona Groarke, born in Edgeworthstown, Co Longford, in 1964, grew up on a farm outside Athlone. Her collections include: *Other People's Houses* (1999), *Flight* (2002) and *Juniper Street* (2006). Awards include the 2003 Michael Hartnett Award. She teaches at the University of Manchester and at Wake Forest University in the US.

Kerry Hardie was born in Singapore in 1951 and grew up in Co Down. Her poetry includes *The Sky Didn't Fall* (2003) and *The Silence Came Close* (2006). Her novels are *Hannie Bennet's Winter Marriage* (2000) and *The Bird Woman* (2006). She received the Kavanagh Fellowship, and The O'Shaughnessy and Michael Hartnett awards. She is a member of Aosdána.

Maurice Harmon is a leading academic and scholar. Poetry collections include: *The Last Regatta* (2000) and *Tales of Death and Other Poems* (2001). He translated *Acallam na Senorach /The Colloquy of Old Men* (2001). Founding editor of the *Irish University Review*, he has published and lectured extensively on literature and bibliography, and edited the now classic *Irish Poetry After Yeats: Seven Poets* (1979). Forthcoming are *Thomas Kinsella: Designing for the Exact Needs* and *The Mischievous Boy and other poems*.

Anne Le Marquand Hartigan, poet, playwright, painter, and mother of six has won many awards for playwriting and poetry. Her plays have been performed in Dublin, Washington DC, Ohio and New Zealand. A sixth poetry collection, *To Keep the Light Burning*, is due in 2008. She has farmed, reared chickens, bred horses – and her ambition is 'to laugh more'. She lives in Dublin.

Dermot Healy was born in Westmeath in 1947. His fiction includes *A Goat's Song* (1994) and *Sudden Times* (1999); his autobiography is *The Bend for Home* (1996). His poetry includes *The Ballyconnel Colours* (1995) and *The Reed Bed* (2001). A member of Aosdána, he lives in Co Sligo.

Seamus Heaney was born in Derry in 1939. Poet, critic, playwright and translator, he received The Nobel Prize for Literature in 1995. His major poetry books include *Door into the Dark*, *North*, *Station Island*, *The Spirit Level*, and *District & Circle* (2007). Prose works include *Preoccupations*, *The Government of the Tongue* and *The Redress of Poetry*. With Ted Hughes, he edited *The Rattle Bag*. He lives in Dublin and is a member of Aosdána.

Rita Ann Higgins was born in 1955 in Galway and left school early to work. Her collections include: *Goddess on the Mervue Bus* (1986), *Philomena's Revenge* (1992) and *An Awful Racket* (2001). She has written four plays. A member of Aosdána, she lives in Galway.

Pat Ingoldsby lives happily in Clontarf with his three cats, Hoot, Rince and Runda, and Barnaby Bish, a goldfish. Together they make up Willow Publications from where his poems appear at a rate of approximately one book each year. He sells them with pride on the streets of Dublin. The rest of his time he is busy opening doors and tins of pet food.

Biddy Jenkinson's books include *Oíche Bhealtaine* (2005) leabhar filíochta, and a book for young persons, illustrated by Ri-bo *An Bhanrion Bess agus Gusai-Gaimbín* (2007). Is maith le Biddy bheith ag filíocht. Is maith léi freisin, feithidí, plandaí agus ainmhithe. Is maith léi amhráin a chanadh ach ní maith le daoine eile bheith ag éisteacht léi …

Fred Johnston was born in Belfast in 1951. His collections include: *True North* (1997), *Being Anywhere - New & Selected Poems* (2001) and *The Oracle Room* (2007). His novels are *Atlanta* (2000) and *The Neon Rose* (2007). He received the Prix de l'Ambassade for translating the French poet, Michel Martin. A regular poetry reviewer for *Books Ireland*, he lives in Galway.

Rita Kelly was born in Galway in 1953. Collections include *An Bealach Eadóigh* (1984), *Fare Well: Beir Beannacht* (1990), and the award-winning *Kelly Reads Bewick* in 2001. She received the Merriman and the Seán Ó Ríordáin Memorial awards, a Kavanagh Fellowship, and won best Irish poem in the 2007 Samhain Poetry Festival.

Brendan Kennelly (b. 1936), from Ballylongford in Kerry, has recently retired from the School of English in Trinity College where he taught for forty-two years. His thirty plus volumes of poetry have won him an international audience. His work includes poetry, plays, novels and critical essays.

Thomas Kinsella, born in Dublin in 1928, retired from the Department of Finance in 1965. His many notable collections include *Butcher's Dozen, Poems From City Centre* and *Madonna and Other Poems*. His translations of *The Táin*, and of Gaelic poems in *An Duanaire* are major contributions to modern poetry. He edited the *New Oxford Book of Irish Verse* (2001); Claddagh has published his CD *Poems 1956—2006*. He received the Freedom of the City of Dublin in 2007. He lives in the USA, returning regularly to Ireland.

Ann Leahy was born in Borrisoleigh, Co Tipperary, and did English at UCD before studying law. She has won the Kavanagh, the Gerard Manley Hopkins and the New Writer (UK) awards. Her first collection, *The Woman who Lived her Life Backwards*, is due in 2008. She lives in Dublin.

Una Leavy was born in Charlestown, Co Mayo. She is author of eight children's books including *The O'Brien Press Book of Irish Fairytales and Legends*, and *Goodbye Pappa*. She teaches in Tavneena National School.

Michael Longley was born in Belfast in 1939. He has published eight collections of poetry including *Gorse Fires* (1991), a Whitbread Poetry Award winner, and *The Weather in Japan* (2000) which won the Hawthornden, the T. S. Eliot and the Irish Times Poetry prizes. His collection, *Snow Water* (2004) won the Librex Montale Prize. *Collected Poems* was published in 2006. He is a Fellow of the Royal Society of Literature, and a member of Aosdána.

Tom Mac Intyre was born in Cavan in 1931. A dual-language writer, his many Abbey Theatre plays include *The Great Hunger* which toured internationally, and *Cúirt An Mheán Oíche/The Midnight Court* (1999). His short fiction *The Harper's Turn* (1982) is introduced by Seamus Heaney, and *The Word for Yes, New and Selected Stories* was published in 1991. Poetry collections include *Fleur-du-Lit* (1994) and *Stories of a Girl* (2003). A member of Aosdána, he lives in Co Cavan.

Catherine Phil MacCarthy was born in Limerick in 1954. A former editor of *Poetry Ireland Review*, her collections include *This Hour of the Tide* (1994) *The Blue Globe* (1998), *Suntrap* (2007) and a first novel, *One Room an Everywhere* (2003). UCD writer-in-residence in 2002, she lives in Dublin.

John McAuliffe grew up in Listowel, Co Kerry and now co-directs the Centre for New Writing in Manchester. His two collections are *A Better Life* (2002) and *Next Door* (2007).

Joan McBreen is from Sligo and lives in Tuam, Co Galway. Her poetry includes *The Wind Beyond the Wall* (1990), *Winter in The Eye – New and Selected Poems* (2003), and *The Long Light on the Land* – Poems with music (on CD, 2004). *Sheltering on Heather Island*, a new collection, is forthcoming. She edited *The White Page – An Bhileog Bhán; Twentieth Century Irish Women Poets* (4th reprint, 2007).

Thomas McCarthy was born in Cappoquin, Co Waterford in 1954. His poetry collections include *Mr Dineen's Careful Parade, New & Selected Poems* (1999). He is also a novelist, and has published a memoir, *The Garden of Remembrance* (1998). *Merchant Prince*, an unusual combination of prose and verse in vividly imagined history, was published in 2005. A winner of the Kavanagh Award, he is a member of Aosdána and lives in Cork.

Terry McDonagh (b. 1946), originally from Cill Aodain, Kiltimagh, Co Mayo has lived in Hamburg for over twenty years. He has published a play, four books of poetry (including *A World Without Stone/New and Selected Poems*, 1998, and in 2003, *A Song for Joanna*), a book of letters, a novel for young people, as well as essays and stories. *Cill Aodáin and Nowhere Else* is due in 2008.

Iggy McGovern was born in Coleraine and lives in Dublin where he is Associate Professor of Physics in Trinity College. His first collection *The King of Suburbia* received the inaugural Glen Dimplex New Writers Award for Poetry.

Medbh McGuckian was born in Belfast in 1950 and her family roots are in the Glens of Antrim. Her poetry includes *The Flower Master* (1982), *Marconi's Cottage* (1991) shortlisted for The Irish Times/Aer Lingus Irish Literature Prize for Poetry, *The Face of the Earth* (2002) and *Had I a Thousand Lives* (2003). She has received several literature awards. A member of Aosdána, she teaches at the Seamus Heaney Centre for Poetry.

Buncrana-born Frank McGuinness is one of Ireland's leading playwrights. His plays include: *The Factory Girls, Observe the Sons of Ulster Marching Towards the Somme, Carthaginians, Someone Who'll Watch Over Me, Mutabilitie, There Came a Gypsy Riding*. His translation of Ibsen's *A Doll's House* won a Tony award in 1997. His poetry includes: *The Stone Jug* (2003) and *Dulse* (2007). He lives in Dublin.

Máighréad Medbh from Newcastle West, Co Limerick claims to have experienced everything she writes about – at least in her dreams. A well-known performance poet at gigs in Ireland, UK and USA, she has three collections: *The Making of a Pagan* (1990), *Tenant* (1999), and *¡Divas!* (2003). A new collection, *When the Air Inhales You*, is due in 2008. She released a CD, *Out of My Skin*, in 2002. She had a five-part story for children on Lyric FM radio in 2007. She lives in Swords, Co Dublin.

Paula Meehan is a Dublin-born poet and playwright. Other work for the young includes stageplays *Kirkle, The Voyage, The Wolf of Winter*. Poetry collections include *Pillow Talk* and *Dharmakaya*. Forthcoming are *Music for Dogs* and *The Wolf Tree*. Her work has been adapted for music, film and dance. She is a member of Aosdána.

Máire Mhac an tSaoi was born in Dublin in 1922. Her main collections are: *Margadh na Saoire* (1956), *Codladh an Ghaiscigh* (1973), *An Galar Dubhach* (1980), and *An Cion go dtí Seo* (1987). *A Heart Full of Thought* is her selection of translations from Classical Gaelic poetry. She won the O'Shaughnessy Poetry Award 1988. Her autobiography, *The Same Age as the State*, was published in 2003. She lives in Howth, Co Dublin.

Áine Miller was born in Cork City. Her first collection, *Goldfish in a Baby Bath*, won the 1992 Kavanagh Award. *Touchwood* was published in 2000. She conducts writing workshops, and lives in Dublin.

Noel Monaghan has published four collections including *Curse of the Birds* (2000) and *The Funeral Game* (2004). He adapted *The Children of Lir* for Livin Dred Theatre (2007). His play, *Broken Cups*, won the PJ O'Connor radio drama award. He has received the ASTI Achievements award for his contribution to literature.

John Montague was born in Brooklyn, New York, in 1929 and reared on the family farm in Co Tyrone. He has received numerous literary prizes and honours. A member of Aosdána, his *Collected Poems* was published in 1995, and *Drunken Sailor* in 2004. Fiction includes *Death of a Chieftain* (1964; 1997) and *The Love Present* (1998). *Company: A Chosen Life* and *The Pear is Ripe* (2007) are his memoirs. He was the first Ireland Professor of Poetry.

Paul Muldoon was born in Co Armagh in 1951. Among his ten collections of poetry are *Moy Sand and Gravel* (2002), for which he won the 2003 Pulitzer Prize for Poetry and, most recently, *Horse Latitudes* (2006). He is Chair of the Lewis Center for the Arts at Princeton and Poetry Editor of the *New Yorker*.

Gerry Murphy was born in Cork city in 1952 and still lives there. His many collections include *Rio de la Plata and All That* (1993), *Torso of an Ex-Girlfriend* (2003), and *End of Part One: New & Selected Poems* (2006).

Richard Murphy was born in Co Galway in 1927, and spent his early years in Sri Lanka. He spent the 1960s in Cleggan – where he restored two Galway Hookers. His poetry includes: *Sailing to an Island*, *The Battle of Aughrim*, *The Price of Stone*, *The Mirror Wall* (1989) and *Collected Poems* (2000). His diaries were published as *The Kick* (2002). He now lives in South Africa.

Paul Murray was born in Newcastle, Co Down, in 1947. He entered the Dominican Order in 1966. His poetry includes: *Rites and Meditations* (1982) a Poetry Ireland Choice; *The Absent Fountain* (1991) and *These Black Stars* (2003). He also wrote *The New Wine of Dominican Spirituality: A Drink Called Happiness* (2006). He lives in Rome.

Eiléan Ní Chuilleanáin was born in Cork in 1942. Her many collections include *Acts and Monuments* (1972) and *The Girl Who Married the Reindeer* (2001). She won the Kavanagh Award (1973) and was nominated for the European Literature Prize in 1992. A member of Aosdána, she lives in Dublin.

Nuala Ní Dhomhnaill was born in Lancashire in 1952, of Irish parents, and was brought up in the Dingle Gaeltacht and in Nenagh, Co Tipperary. Collections include *Rogha Dánta/Selected Poems* (1986), *Pharaoh's Daughter* (1990), *Feis* (1991) and *The 50-Minute Mermaid* (2007). She has plays for children including *Jimín* and *An Ollphiast Ghrána*. Awards include Duais Sheáin Uí Ríordáin and Gradam an Oireachtais. Appointed a Naughton Fellow (2006-07) at Notre Dame University, she is a member of Aosdána and lives in Co Dublin.

Tipperary-born Áine Ní Ghlinn's most recent collection is *Unshed Tears/ Deora Nár Caoineadh* (1996). Her children's books include *Daifní Díneasár* (2001) *Moncaí Dána* (2002), *Céard tá sa Bhosca* (2001) which won the American Clann Lir award, and *Éasca Péasca* (2007). She lives in Dublin.

Colette Nic Aodha lives in Galway with her three children and works as a teacher in Headford. Her published poetry includes: *Faoi Chrann Cnó Capaill* (2000), *Gallúnach ar Rópa* (2003), *Sundial* (2005), *Between Curses/Bainne Giar* (2006) and short stories.

Mícheál Ó Conghaile founded the Cló Iar-Chonnachta publishing house in 1985. His writing includes poetry, short stories, a novel, a play, and a novella, and some translation. He has won the Hennessy Award, and was shortlisted for the Irish Times Literary Awards for his novel *Sna Fir*; his play *Cúigear Chonamara* won the Stewart Parker/BBC Ulster Award.

Mícheál Ó Ruairc was born in Brandon, Tralee, Co Kerry, in 1953, and now lives in Dublin. He has several prose books including *An bhFaca Éinne agaibh Roy Keane?* (2003). His poetry volumes are *Fuil Samhraidh* (1987), *Loco in Lios na Caolbhaí* (2001), and in English, *Humane Killing* (1992).

Cathal Ó Searcaigh is from Donegal and lives at the foot of Mount Errigal. His poetry includes *Gúru i gClúidíní* (2006), *Na Buachaillí Bána* (1995) and *Ag Tnúth leis an tSolas* (2001) which received the Irish Times Irish Literature Prize. He won the Seán Ó Ríordáin Prize for Poetry and Duais Bhord na Gaeilge. He is a member of Aosdána.

Julie O'Callaghan, born in 1954 in Chicago, has lived in Ireland since 1974. Her latest book for adults is *Tell Me This Is Normal: New and Selected Poems* (2008). Children's collections are: *Taking My Pen For A Walk* (1988), *Two Barks* (1998) and *The Book of Whispers* (2006). She lives in Kildare and is a member of Aosdána.

Ulick O'Connor was born in Dublin in 1929. Biographer, playwright, poet, and sportsman, his plays include *The Grand Inquisitor, Deirdre, A Trinity of Two, Joycity and Executions*. *Irish Tales and Sagas* appeared in 1981. Poetry collections include *Poems of the Damned*, translations from Baudelaire (1991). His biographies of Gogarty and Behan are the standard works. Other works include: *Diaries, 1970-1981* (2003) and *Laugh at Gilded Butterflies: A Selection of Favourite Poems* (2007). He is a member of Aosdána and lives in Dublin.

Mary O'Donnell writes poetry and fiction. She has five collections of poetry, most recently, *The Place of Miracles* (new & selected, 2006). She is a poetry mentor with Carlow University Pittsburgh's MFA in Creative Writing. Her first novel *The Light-Makers* was Sunday Tribune Best New Irish Novel, 1992; other novels are *Virgin and the Boy* and *The Elysium Testament* (1999). A short story collection *Strong Pagans* appeared in 1991. She is a member of Aosdána.

John O'Donnell, born 1960, has been published widely and has broadcast on RTE. Awards include the Hennessy/Sunday Tribune Poetry Award. He has two volumes of poetry: *Some Other Country* (2002) and *Icarus Sees His Father Fly* (2004). He lives in Dublin.

Ciaran O'Driscoll was born in Callan, Co Kilkenny, in 1943. His has five collections, including *Moving On, Still There: New and Selected Poems* (2001). He also published a childhood memoir, *A Runner Among Falling Leaves*, in 2001. He received the Kavanagh Fellowship in Poetry in 2000. He lives in Limerick and is a member of Aosdána.

Dennis O'Driscoll was born in Thurles in 1954. His eight books of poetry include: *Weather Permitting* (1999) a Poetry Book Society Recommendation and shortlisted for the Irish Times Poetry Prize; *Exemplary Damages* (2002); *New and Selected Poems* (2004) a Poetry Book Society Special Commendation; and *Reality Check* (2007 & USA 2008). He edited the *Bloodaxe Book of Poetry Quotations* (2006). His many awards include the Lannan Literary Award, the E.M. Forster Award (American Academy of Arts and Letters), and the O'Shaughnessy Award for Poetry (2006). A member of Aosdána, he has worked as a civil servant since the age of 16.

Desmond O'Grady was born in Limerick in 1935 and spent many years travelling and teaching – London, Rome, America, Egypt, Greece. His many poetry collections include: *The Headgear of the Tribe, The Road Taken: Collected Poems 1950-1996; Kurdish Poems of Love & Liberty*, trans (2005); *On My Way*, and *My Alexandria* (both 2006); *Ten Modern Arab Poets* trans. (2007). He now lives in Kinsale, Co Cork.

Aislinn O'Loughlin co-authored the popular children's verse collection *Worms Can't Fly*. She wrote several whacky alternative tales for children including *Cinderella's Fella, A Right Royal Pain*, an international White Ravens citation, and *Fionn the Cool*. She lives in Dublin.

Larry O'Loughlin is a storyteller and author of books for younger children, such as *The Gobán Saor*, and for teenagers, such as *Is Anybody Listening* – both shortlisted for the Bisto Book for the Year. *Breaking the Silence* (2001) is a groundbreaking young adult novel. He received White Raven citations (International Youth Library Association) for both his teen novels. He co-authored *Worms Can't Fly* with his daughter Aislinn (qv). He lives in Templeogue, Co Dublin. His poem here was composed with the aid of the children of St Thomas' School, Jobstown, Tallaght.

Nessa O'Mahony was born in Dublin and lives there. She has published two poetry collections, *Bar Talk* (1999) and *Trapping a Ghost* (2005), and *The Side Road to Star* is forthcoming. She received an Arts Council Literature Bursary in 2004 and a South Dublin County Council Bursary in 2007. She has a PhD in Creative Writing from the University of Bangor.

Mary O'Malley was born in Connemara, Co Galway. Her collections include *Where the Rocks Float* (1993), *The Knife in the Wave* (1997), *Asylum Road* (2001), *The Boning Hall* (2002) and *A Perfect V* (2007). She received a Hennessy Award in 1990. A member of Aosdána, she lives in Connemara.

Caitriona O'Reilly is a poet and critic. Her first collection *The Nowhere Birds* (2001) won the Rooney Prize for Irish Literature; *The Sea Cabinet* (2006) was a Poetry Book Society Recommendation and shortlisted for the Irish Times Poetry Now Prize. She lives and works in Dublin.

Micheal O'Siadhail was born in Dublin in 1947. His twelfth collection *Globe* was published in 2007; other collections are *Love Life* (2005), *The Gossamer Wall: Poems in Witness to the Holocaust* (2002) and *Poems 1975-1995* (1995). Awarded an Irish American Cultural Institute Prize (1982), a Toonder Prize (1998) and shortlisted for Wingate Jewish Quarterly Prize (2003). He is a member of Aosdána.

Frank Ormsby was born in Enniskillen, Co Fermanagh, in 1947 and studied at Queen's University, Belfast. He teaches at the Royal Belfast Academical Institution where he is Head of English. He was editor of *The Honest Ulsterman* for twenty years, and compiled *Poets from the North of Ireland* (1979) and *A Rage for Order: Poetry of the NI Troubles* (1992). His collections include *Northern Spring* (1986) and *The Ghost Train* (1996).

Justin Quinn was born in Dublin in 1968 and now lives in Prague. He has published four books of poetry, most recently *Waves & Trees* (2006).

Al Reza was born in 1978 and lives in Dublin. He has only recently begun submitting poetry for publication. He also works at graphic design, illustration and painting.

Maurice Riordan was born in Lisgoold, Co Cork, in 1953. His collections are: *A Word from the Loki* (1995), a Poetry Book Society Choice, *Floods* (2000) and *The Holy Land* (2007). He received the Michael Hartnett Award in 2007.

Mark Roper won the 1992 Aldeburgh Prize for best first collection with *The Hen Ark*. Other volumes are: *Catching the Light* (1997) and *The Home Fire* (1998). A 'New & Selected' volume is due in 2008. He edited *Poetry Ireland Review* in 1999.

Gabriel Rosenstock was born in Kilfinane, Co Limerick, in 1949. He writes primarily in Irish and has published over one hundred books. *Rogha Rosenstock* (1994) is a selection of his poetry. His children's poetry is selected as *Dánta Duitse* (1998). He lives in Dublin and is a member of Aosdána.

John W Sexton's most recent poetry collections are *Vortex* (2005) and *Petit Mal* (2008). Scriptwriter for RTE's children's radio show *The Ivory Tower*, his novels *The Johnny Coffin Diaries* and *Johnny Coffin School-Dazed* are based on this series. He was awarded a Kavanagh Fellowship in Poetry (2007) and is currently Fiction Editor of the *Cork Literary Review*.

Jo Slade's poetry collections include *In Fields I Hear Them Sing* (1989), *The Vigilant One* (1994), *City of Bridges* (2005), and an English and French version of her *Selected Poems: Certain Octobers* (1997). She lives in Limerick.

Michael Smith was born in Dublin in 1942. In 1967 he founded New Writers' Press which published neglected modernist poets, as well as numerous younger poets. He was also founder editor of *The Lace Curtain* journal. His many volumes include *With the Woodnymphs* (1968), *The Purpose of Gift: Selected Poems* (1985) and *Meditations on Metaphors* (1998). He received the European Academy of Poetry Medal in 2001 for poetry translation. He lives in Dublin.

Sydney Bernard Smith was born in Glasgow in 1936 and raised in Portstewart, Co Derry. His work has been broadcast widely and staged in Ireland, at the Edinburgh Festival and in the US. His poetry collections include *New and Selected Poems* (1984). Plays include *How to Roast a Strasbourg Goose* (1985) and he published a novel, *Flannery* (1991). He lives in Dundalk and is a member of Aosdána.

Dubliner Gerard Smyth began publishing poetry in the late 1960s. His work has appeared in Ireland and abroad in journals, and in translation. The most recent of six collections are *A New Tenancy* (2004) and *The Mirror Tent* (2007).

Matthew Sweeney was born Co Donegal in 1952. Publications for children include *Up on the Roof: New & Selected Poems* (2001), and a novel, *Fox* (2002). He is editor of *The New Faber Book of Children's Poems* (2001). His latest collection (for adults) is *Sanctuary* (2004). He is currently Writer in Residence at the Munster Literature Centre and spends time in Donegal and Berlin.

Eamonn Wall was born in Enniscorthy, Co Wexford, in 1955. He is the author of four collections, most recently *Refuge at DeSoto Bend* (2004). His prose includes *From the Sin-é Café to the Black Hills, Notes on the New Irish* (2000). He now lives and teaches in St. Louis, Missouri.

Grace Wells lives with her partner and her two children in Co Tipperary. She has written children's novels: *Ice Dreams* (2008), and *Gyrfalcon* (2002) which won the Eilis Dillon Memorial Award.

Joseph Woods was born in 1966 in Drogheda. He is Director of Poetry Ireland. In 2000 he won the Patrick Kavanagh Award. His collections are *Sailing to Hokkaido* (2001) and *Bearings* (2005).

Macdara Woods was born in Dublin in 1942. A co-editor and founder of *Cyphers*, he is a member of Aosdána. His sixteen books, mostly poetry, as well as CDs and musical collaborations include *Knowledge in the Blood*, (2000, reissued 2007), *The Nightingale Water* (2000), *Artichoke Wine* (2006).

Adam Wyeth, from Sussex, now lives near Kinsale. He was runner-up in the Arvon International poetry Competition, 2007 and selected for the Poetry Ireland Introductions Series, 2007. He published *The Wandering Celt*, a CD of readings by Desmond O'Grady (qv). He teaches creative writing in Cork.

Enda Wyley was born in Dublin 1966. Her collections of poetry are *Eating Baby Jesus* (1993), *Socrates in the Garden* (1998) and *Poems for Breakfast* (2004). She has published for young readers *Boo and Bear* (2003) and a children's novel, *The Silver Notebook*, (2007).

INDEX OF FIRST LINES

INDEX OF POEMS

INDEX OF POETS AND ILLUSTRATORS

The Illustrators

Corrina Askin 14, 15, 18, 19, 22, 23, 30, 31, 34, 35, 36, 37, 40, 41, 49, 50, 51, 54, 55, 56, 57, 60, 61, 64, 65, 68, 69, 70, 71, 76, 77, 84, 85, 86, 87, 90, 91, 92, 93, 97, 98, 99, 106, 107, 112, 113, 118, 119, 120, 121, 124, 130, 131, 140, 141, 144, 145, 148, 149, 150

Emma Byrne 11, 12, 13, 20, 21, 24, 82, 83, 104, 105, 125, 126, 127

Alan Clarke 16, 17, 25, 26, 27, 28, 29, 32, 33, 38, 39, 42, 43, 44, 45, 46, 52, 53, 58, 59, 62, 63, 66, 67, 72, 73, 74, 75, 78, 79, 80, 81, 88, 89, 94, 100, 101, 102, 103, 108, 109, 110, 111, 114, 115, 116, 117, 122, 123, 128, 129, 132, 133, 134, 135, 136, 137, 138, 139, 142, 143, 146, 147

First published 2004 by The O'Brien Press Ltd,
12 Terenure Road East, Rathgar, Dublin 6, Ireland.
Tel: +353 1 4923333; Fax: +353 1 4922777
E-mail: books@obrien.ie; Website: www.obrien.ie
Reprinted 2008.

ISBN: 978-1-84717-092-7
First published in hardback 2004.
This paperback edition first published 2008.

British Library Cataloguing-in-publication Data
Something beginning with P : new poems from Irish poets
1. Children's poetry, English - Irish authors 2. Children's poetry, Irish
I. Cashman, Seamus II. Askin, Corrina III. Clarke, Alan
821.9'140809415

2 3 4 5 6 7 8 9 10
08 09 10 11 12

The O'Brien Press receives assistance from
The Arts Council/An Chomairle Ealaíon

The O'Brien Press acknowledges assistance for this project from
The Arts Council of Northern Ireland

EDITOR'S ACKNOWLEDGMENTS
For permission to source some biographical data from his Irish Writers Online website, my thanks to Philip Casey; and for assistance with translation many thanks to Diarmuid Ó Cathasaigh, and the individual poets. However, any errors ensuing are entirely my responsibility. To all the poets who are represented in this volume, my sincere thanks and appreciation for cooperation throughout the process of commissioning, editing and proofing the work. I was very pleased to renew contact with many poet friends I have had the pleasure of publishing in book or anthology over the years, and delighted to have also now made contact with so many other writers whose poetry I had read and admired. Poetry Ireland, in particular Joe and Sara, provided much valuable contact information and I am grateful for their enthusiasm for this project. To Íde and Emma at The O'Brien Press my admiration and gratitude for editorial and design advice, direction and wisdom. And to The O'Brien Press whose idea the book was, and Poetry Ireland for endorsing and supporting it, my thanks for giving me the pleasure of commissioning and editing it.

PUBLISHER'S ACKNOWLEDGEMENTS
Several people and organisations helped with this innovative publishing project. Above, the editor acknowledges those who assisted him. Our greatest appreciation to the editor, the poets and illustrators, all of whom brought great flair, thoughtfulness and artistry to the project. We appreciate the support of the Arts Councils, south and north. Our special thanks to Joe Woods and Jane O'Hanlon of Poetry Ireland, and to RTÉ for their generous support and their true appreciation of the value of this work.

Layout, typesetting, design, editing: The O'Brien Press Ltd.
Printing: KHL Singapore